They Were All Statues . . .

A natural pool curved in a crescent that reflected the fiery sky and rippled lazily in the breeze. Beside it stood another of the magnificent carvings, this one of a life-size unicorn caught in the act of lifting his head from the pond. A Viking warrior stood beside him, one powerful hand resting on the creature's back. Kareth found herself touched by the beauty of his form in a way no work of art had ever before moved her.

At that moment the Viking turned his head toward her and smiled. "If you want to watch me work, you should come closer."

Kareth's mouth dropped open in surprise and her heart beat a wild tattoo in the vicinity of her throat. "Are you real?" she demanded fearfully.

LYNDA TRENT

started writing at the insistence of a friend, but it was her husband who provided moral support whenever her resolve flagged. Now, as she puts it, "Both he and I are award-winning writers and love it."

Dear Reader:

SILHOUETTE DESIRE is an exciting new line of contemporary romances from Silhouette Books. During the past year, many Silhouette readers have written in telling us what other types of stories they'd like to read from Silhouette, and we've kept these comments and suggestions in mind in developing SILHOUETTE DESIRE.

DESIREs feature all of the elements you like to see in a romance, plus a more sensual, provocative story. So if you want to experience all the excitement, passion and joy of falling in love, then SILHOUETTE DESIRE is for you.

For more details write to:

Jane Nicholls
Silhouette Books
PO Box 236
Thornton Road
Croydon
Surrey CR9 3RU

LYNDA TRENT
The Enchantment

Silhouette Desire

Originally Published by Silhouette Books
division of
Harlequin Enterprises Ltd.

First published in Great Britain 1985 by Silhouette Books, 15–16 Brook's Mews, London W1A 1DR

© Dan Trent and Lynda Trent 1985

Silhouette, Silhouette Desire and Colophon are Trade Marks of Harlequin Enterprises B.V.

ISBN 0 373 05201 4

22–1085

Made and printed in Great Britain by Richard Clay (The Chaucer Press) Ltd, Bungay, Suffolk

To Gina Haldane,
who knows about the unicorns

The
Enchantment

1

Kareth Langley muttered an expletive under her breath as the black-topped road dwindled to hard-packed dirt. She had taken the wrong turn again; she knew she had. Rolling down the dusty window, she looked around at the surrounding woods, but this gave her no further clue as to where she might be. Enormous pines speared the late afternoon sky and in their midst pale dogwoods seemed to float like an army of ghosts. Giant wisterias threaded among the arching sweet gums and budding oaks and the vivid purple clusters of their flowers lent an intense sweetness to the air. But nowhere did she see a road sign that would set her on the right track toward her destination.

A glance at the lowering sun told Kareth she had

about an hour of daylight left. For the first time she felt a shiver of concern. Darkness in the Texas countryside was nothing at all like its counterpart in town. When night fell here it would be pitch black. If she didn't find her way out in daylight, it would be impossible after dark.

The road had become progressively more narrow with each mile she had come from the main highway and was now scarcely wider than a single lane. Deep ditches bordered both sides and beyond them was the virtually impenetrable tangle of the Big Thicket. She couldn't chance getting her car stuck trying to turn around, so she had no choice but to drive on and hope she would find a safer place to do so.

Kareth rolled up the window and continued down the hard-packed dirt road. Behind her the wheels whipped up a cloud of dust that filmed her car and obscured her view of where she had been. The trees reached over the road and the limbs swayed toward one another as if their leafy fingers sought to catch her. Kareth shoved down the fanciful image. They were only trees moving with the breeze and this was only a road. Nothing else.

The car lurched, then steadied, then jerked again. Kareth frowned at the row of gauges and her heart plummeted. The needle on the fuel indicator was quivering on the small red E. Even as she looked, the car coughed again and slowed to a stop. Kareth took her foot off the accelerator and glared at the gas gauge as she chastised herself for not checking it before leaving Livingston.

The billows of dust caught up with her and settled in beige shadows over the car she had washed only that morning. Kareth closed her eyes and tried to keep from panicking. She couldn't be as badly lost as she thought. After all, she had not come that far from where she turned off the county road, and now that the dust had settled, she could see tire tracks on the surface ahead. That meant someone had driven through here. She had only to wait for rescue.

Glancing at her watch, Kareth narrowed her silver eyes thoughtfully. Less than an hour until sundown. The farmer that used this road might go to town only once a week and she couldn't wait days for him to happen by. She was terrified of the idea of even spending the night here. Helplessly she thought of all the chores waiting for her at the television station. There was a tape to edit from her recent interview with a blacksmith. She had notes to file about leads for the next month's shows, not to mention the fan mail she needed to answer. She didn't have *time* to be stranded in the Big Thicket.

The ridiculousness of the thought made her smile —as if she would have scheduled this in had she only known.

Kareth gazed out the window, blinked, and leaned forward. There at the turn of the road was a path such as would lead to a farmhouse. After a second's pause she opened her car door and got out. A stray breeze lifted her whiskey-colored hair and swept it back from her shoulders. A house might be just beyond those trees.

Resolutely, she locked her car door and slipped the thin strap of her purse over her shoulder. Luckily she had no expensive camera equipment to leave unguarded or to lug along. She had been on her way to set up an interview rather than to tape it. The woman she was hoping to find had no phone. Kareth refused to even think that the farmhouse she hoped to find might not have one either.

The dirt beneath her low-heeled shoes was soft and felt warm from the spring sunshine, but already the air held the cool of approaching night. Kareth consulted her watch and decided she would walk for twenty minutes. If she had not found someone by then, she could still find her way back to the car before dark.

The path led into the thick woods. Tiny violets sprinkled the trail and small white flowers lay like scattered stardust in drifts about the mossy trunks. Leaves from countless seasons made the ground spongy, and in the distance Kareth heard a mockingbird's lilting song.

Once she was within the forest it was much darker. Twilight had already fallen beneath the thick dome of leaves. The wisteria's scent was heavy here where the air moved little, if at all. She tried not to notice that the dogwoods looked even more like ghosts now that she was alone with them. But Kareth was not one to run from her fears, so she hastened her steps and continued. The sooner she found someone, the quicker she could be on her way back to town.

The path curved deeper into the forest. Huge logs draped with emerald moss and dotted with wedges of fan-shaped fungus lay by the path. Chalky mushrooms flourished in fairy circles and tall ferns made patches of vivid green lace. Through the leaves Kareth could see the rosy hue of the sky as it deepened to purple. In another ten minutes she would have to head back.

She rounded a sharp curve and came to an abrupt halt, her heart pounding wildly. Ahead stood an enormous Viking warrior in full battle dress. A helmet crowned his head and his fierce eyes seemed to bore straight through her. In one hand he held a shield and in the other a massive battle-ax.

Kareth blinked to chase away the hallucination, but the Viking stood his ground, utterly motionless. Swallowing against the lump in her throat, Kareth edged closer. To her vast relief she realized that she was looking at an extremely lifelike statue. No, not a statue, she corrected herself as she approached the giant warrior, but a wood carving. The Viking had been fashioned from a huge tree whose roots were still firmly planted in the earth.

Now that her fear was gone, Kareth touched the smooth wood with wonder. Who had carved it, and why? She looked around. Farther down the path she saw two more figures. These were much smaller and appeared to be gnomes that were pointing the way down one fork in the path.

Feeling as if she had stumbled through Alice's looking glass, Kareth followed the direction the gnomes indicated. The trees were farther apart here, giving the appearance of a primeval park. Without the wooden gnomes as signposts, she might have taken the other path and missed all this. Gigantic pines stretched into the sunset sky and the woods' floor was carpeted in golden needles that whispered under her feet. Above her a gentle breeze caressed the boughs, wafting a heady aroma among the trees.

As she left the pines and entered a grove of hardwood trees, the underbush became more dense and again the path narrowed. Suddenly the trees thinned and Kareth found herself at the edge of a small meadow filled with enchantment.

A natural pool curved in a crescent that reflected the fiery sky and rippled lazily in the breeze. Beside it stood another of the magnificent carvings, this one of a life-size unicorn caught in the act of lifting his head from the pond. Another of the Vikings stood beside him, a powerful hand resting on the creature's back. This one wore no shirt and smooth muscles corded his remarkable body. Kareth found herself touched by the beauty of his form in a way no work of art had ever before moved her.

At the center of the meadow was a large toadstool

with three ethereal fairies playing around it, one in the motion of leapfrogging over the top. A deer and her fawn, carved from reddish-hued cedar, stood poised for flight at the far edge of the clearing.

Kareth was so spellbound at the unexpected sights that she completely forgot her need to hurry. In the growing twilight she could almost believe the figures were alive.

At that moment the Viking turned his head toward her and smiled. "If you want to watch me work, you should come closer."

Kareth's mouth dropped open in surprise and her heart beat a wild tattoo in the vicinity of her throat. "Are you real?" she demanded fearfully.

The man laughed and turned back to the unicorn. A faint burr sounded as he ran sandpaper over the sleek wooden neck. "Of course I am. Are you?" He glanced back at her. "You aren't dressed much like a wood nymph, but then, I haven't seen one lately. Maybe their clothing styles have changed."

Her fear melted as she walked into the clearing. Feeling rather foolish, she said, "I guess the carvings were playing on my imagination. At first I thought you were one of them."

She was close enough now to wonder how she had ever mistaken this man for a statue. His body exuded vitality, and his charisma was almost a tangible substance. His hair was pale gold and was ruffled boyishly. Eyes as green as the needles of the pines, fringed by long lashes of the darkest gold, held a clear-sighted intelligence. His features were handsome—no other word could adequately describe them—and would have done credit to an artist. Lean muscles flowed beneath his tanned skin and veins curved over his powerful forearms and square hands. On stepping closer, Kareth saw that he wore faded jeans and tennis shoes that did nothing to detract from his perfection. Rather, it was as if they were part of him, as the unicorn had a mane and the fairies had wings.

Realizing she was staring and that he knew it, she looked away abruptly. "I admire your work," she said in what she hoped was a businesslike tone. "I don't believe I've ever seen it in a gallery or any of the shows around here."

"No, I can't say that you would have." His green eyes met hers and she saw amusement in their depths. "People don't usually come way out here to tell me that, however."

Kareth looked away, her usual composure ruffled. "I'm here by accident. I mean, my car is out of gas and I'm lost. That is, first I was lost and then I ran out of gas." She groaned inwardly at her nervous rambling. "I apologize for trespassing on your land but I saw the path and thought there might be a house where I could call for help." She looked around uncertainly. "There *is* a house, isn't there?"

He was regarding her with interest. "Yes, I have a house. Did you expect me to live in a hollow tree?"

"No, of course not. I didn't mean to invade your privacy, but . . ."

"I know, you're lost and out of gas. You said that." His eyes flicked from her face to the path and back again. "You're lucky you found me. I don't think there's another farm within ten miles."

"You're right. I haven't seen anything but trees in the last half hour of driving." She paused. What made her so sure she could trust this man? She had spent too many years in cities to be able to casually converse with a half-naked stranger in the middle of the woods.

He seemed totally impervious to her nervousness. Instead, he bent and picked up his bag of tools and slung them over his shoulder. "It's getting too dark to work anyway. Come on up to the house."

Kareth's eyes met his and she felt almost dizzy—as if for a second their souls had touched. "Do you have a phone?" she asked breathlessly as she tried to quell the stirring in the middle of her stomach.

"Of course." He grinned. "I even have electricity and indoor plumbing."

A rare blush colored her cheeks. "Everyone doesn't. I was on my way to interview a midwife who has neither a phone nor electricity." She smiled and added, "I don't know about the plumbing."

An answering smile curved his lips. "I wouldn't count on it. What are you, a newspaper reporter?"

Kareth felt oddly provoked. Her show might not

be a nationwide syndication, but she had a lot of viewers. "I'm in television. I do the 'Texas Lifestyles' show." When he gave no sign of recognition, she said, "I'm Kareth Langley, the emcee."

"Kareth," he repeated. "I like that. I don't watch much television." He turned to walk across the clearing, the bag of tools still slung over his back.

"Wait," she called out. "I don't know your name."

He paused and looked back at her. The last fingers of sunlight rimmed his powerful body and made a pale glow in his light hair. More than ever Kareth was reminded of a mythical Viking. "My name is Lake. Lake Thorsen."

Again his sensitive lips tilted upward and Kareth was keenly aware of a fluttering sensation in her middle. "Your w-wife," she stammered as he again turned away. "Will she mind if I use the phone?"

He looked back. "I don't have a wife. I live alone."

Kareth could feel the current pass between them. Although several yards of grass separated them, she felt enfolded in his charisma.

"Will your husband worry about you?" he asked softly.

Slowly she shook her head. "I'm not married either."

"Do you also live alone?"

Kareth found herself nodding, all her city training dissolving under his hypnotic gaze.

A cricket sang in the waving grass and was answered by another in the trees. Above them two birds flew in black silhouette against the ruddy sky in search of a roost for the night.

"If you want to use the phone, you'll have to come with me," he reminded her. "The cord won't reach this far."

Kareth jerked back to reality and hurried after him. Lake waited until she was near, then strode out across the meadow. He led her up a path much like the one she had traveled earlier. Darkness was falling fast now and she had to watch carefully to keep from tripping.

They crossed a small bridge of rough-hewn logs and she gasped at the sight of a form squatting in its shadows.

Lake laughed. "It's only the bridge troll. He's carved of cypress. Over there is a dragon, but it's too dark to see him very well."

Kareth peered through the dusk and made out the ridges of an enormous curving back and tail. She hurried to catch up with Lake.

The path broadened and became wide enough for two people to walk side by side. Lightning bugs glimmered and vanished in the night-shadowed bushes and an owl hooted in the distance.

"Are you sure you have a house?" Kareth asked as she hurried to keep up with his long strides.

"Sure I do. It's right there." He pointed toward the clearing ahead. On the far side of the opening was a two-story log building that blended so well into the woods that flanked it, Kareth wasn't surprised she hadn't seen it for herself. The deep porch that skirted two sides held an old-fashioned porch swing as well as several redwood chairs. The lawn was strewn with a profusion of bluebonnets and other wild flowers, and a spreading oak sheltered the house.

Feeling an awe that closely resembled the sensation she had felt in the meadow, Kareth followed Lake onto the porch. He reached inside to flip on the switch and the porch was flooded with a yellow light.

"See? Electricity. Just as I promised." Another click sent light into the hall.

Kareth entered and looked around. Bare logs made up the front and back walls of the large room, but the other two were conventional plaster walls papered in a decidedly masculine dark blue pattern. The stairway to the rooms above, flanked by a glossy oak railing, was carpeted with a deep red runner of an Oriental design. The floor was bare wood but gleamed from obvious care.

"The phone is in here," Lake said as he moved to the room on the left. "Over there on the table. Make yourself at home."

Kareth went into the cozy room. Again there were the logs on the outer walls and paper—this time a forest green and cream design—on the inner partitions. A large throw rug that looked as if it were hand loomed warmed the broad plank floor. A huge fireplace of natural stone dominated the opposite wall. Kareth sat in an overstuffed chair and dialed a number while Lake knelt to start a fire.

Kareth found it difficult to look away from Lake as he bent over his task. His hard muscles rippled smoothly and the fire he was coaxing to life made ruddy gold lights on his skin and hair. He looked like a pagan god clad in jeans. When a voice came over the phone, Kareth jumped.

"Peg, it's me, Kareth. No, I'm not at home. I was on my way to interview that midwife and I ran out of gas." She paused, then covered the receiver with her palm as she asked Lake, "Where am I?"

"You're about twelve miles southeast of Livingston," he answered over his shoulder. "Ask her if she knows how to get to Lanewood."

"Lanewood? I never heard of it."

"It's not there anymore, but this is the road that leads to where it was."

Doubtfully, Kareth turned back to the phone. "Peg, have you ever heard of Lanewood?" She looked over at Lake. "What else are we near?"

He thought for a minute. "Nothing."

"Well, how am I supposed to get back to town?" she asked in exasperation.

"I can get gasoline for you tomorrow."

The crackle of the fire broke the silence. Then Kareth spoke into the receiver. "Peg, ask Jeff if he knows how to get to Lanewood. He's not home? Fishing for two days! Who else can I call?" She frowned as she glanced over at Lake and said, "I don't think that's such a good idea, Peg. No, I can't call him either. If he finds out I got lost, he may have second thoughts about my dependability and cancel my show. You know how closely Mr. Alred is watching me, Peg." With a sigh she said, "I'll be home tomorrow." As an inspiration she added, "If I don't call you by ten o'clock, start looking for me. It's the old Lanewood road and I took a path near my car. 'Bye."

Lake was watching her with interest. "Your friend couldn't help?"

"She doesn't know of the road and her husband is out of town." She stood and shouldered her purse. "I'll go back to the car and wait for morning."

"Why would you do that? You can have the guest room."

Kareth eyed him suspiciously. "I'd feel safer in the car. Not that I mean to insult you, Mr. Thorsen, but it wouldn't look right if I accepted your offer."

"Lake. Wouldn't look right to whom? Unless I'm mistaken, your friend suggested you sleep here."

"I'm sure she assumes I'm with a family. Not alone in the back of nowhere with a strange man."

He grinned and his strong white teeth gleamed. "Do you plan to ravish me?"

"Certainly not!" she gasped.

"Then why do you assume I have the same plans for you?"

The mantel clock ticked the seconds before she said, "I never suggested that you would attack me. I was speaking entirely of appearances."

He stood and hooked his thumbs in the pockets of his jeans. "It's a long walk back to your car and it's dark. Besides, I don't think it's safe for a beautiful woman to sleep alone beside a road in a stranded car. Please stay here."

She felt her pulse race. Other men had called her beautiful. Why did it matter to her that he had done the same? After all, her physical appearance was a tool of her trade, so to speak, for without good features she would never have been allowed her own show. Yet the casual compliment touched her.

"There's a lock on the bedroom door and you will have your own bath," he added as an inducement. "I doubt your car has one."

She smiled and admitted, "You're right. Do you promise the door has a lock?"

"I swear it," he said solemnly.

"All right. I'll stay."

"Good. How about some supper?" Without waiting for her answer, he turned to leave the room.

She had to hurry to catch up. "Don't go to any trouble for me."

"No trouble. I'm making tuna sandwiches."

A few minutes later they sat on the porch, eating sandwiches and crunching tortilla chips. Lake had pulled on a soft blue sweatshirt that in Kareth's eyes made him even more devastatingly handsome. He had loaned her a zip-up sweatshirt against the cool of the night and she felt surprisingly comfortable in it. It was sizes too big and she had to push the sleeves up to expose her hands, but it was fleecy and smelled faintly of his woodsy aftershave.

Lake Thorsen was an enigma, to say the least. Though he lived all alone out here and seemed to be very comfortable doing so, he didn't appear to be a loner or a recluse. People who chose isolation usually insisted that they be allowed to remain that way, but this man had welcomed her with the ease and self-assurance of a practiced host. In fact, why was this very handsome, witty, and talented man unattached?

When Kareth realized the direction her thoughts had turned, she silently chastised herself. The man's personal life was, indeed, none of her business. But his professional life was a different matter. After all, she was an investigative reporter of sorts, and had an obligation to her job and the station to find new material for her program.

"Why do you live here? In the middle of the woods, I mean," Kareth asked without preamble.

Lake studied the night beyond the porch for a while. Then he answered, "This is my home. I've spent most of my life here. My mother was a writer and my father was an artist, so we lived here. He had a log cabin built because it seemed more appropriate to this setting than a conventional house. I went to school in Livingston. This is my home."

"But your sculpture is magnificent. That Viking warrior nearly scared the life out of me."

"He was supposed to. He's my watchdog, I guess you'd say."

"Where do you exhibit? I can't figure out why I haven't heard of you." Recalling her own discomfort at not being recognized, she amended, "Not that I'm an expert in the field of sculpture."

"There's no reason you should recognize me. I don't exhibit anywhere."

Kareth leaned forward. "What? Did you say you don't show your work?"

"That's right. I do it for my own pleasure."

Gently she said, "There would be quite a bit of money if you did. I'm sure you would be very successful."

Lake shrugged and sipped his soft drink. "I don't need the money."

Kareth sat back in astonishment. How could he say that? Here he was, living in a log house in the middle of the Big Thicket and he didn't think he needed the money? "You're kidding," she heard herself gasp. "Everybody needs money."

"What would I buy that I don't already have? I have plenty of everything I need. Actually I live pretty simply. My wood comes from trees that grow right here. My car is in good shape. My house is paid for. If I want to swim, I have a pond nearby. No, I don't need it."

"What kind of an attitude is that?" she demanded.

"A sensible one, I think."

He had leaned back and his face was in the

shadows, but she suspected he was laughing at her. She bit into her sandwich and swallowed before she said, "Well, if you don't need the money, what about your responsibility to the world of art?"

"My what?"

"You're very good. Maybe even a genius! You owe it to people to share your work with them."

"No, I don't."

Kareth stared at him. She didn't consider herself to be any more crass and commercial than the next person, but she couldn't even comprehend his attitude. "Yes, you do."

"Why?"

She couldn't think of a reason. This was the sort of thing that was never questioned. "If a person has a talent, he ought to share it. Let others enjoy it."

"Why?" he repeated.

Kareth was wordless. Finally she managed an inane "Because."

"Not good enough. The world has plenty of art to look at or to trade or sell. Museums are full to overflowing. Art galleries are the same. I've never seen a town that couldn't boast of at least one local artist. The world can live without sculpture by Lake Thorsen."

"That's it!" she crowed triumphantly. "You tried to sell and were rejected! You can't let one or two failures get you down. Why, some artists try for years before they succeed."

"I wasn't rejected. No one has ever seen my

sculptures unless they came here to visit. Or wandered in off the road."

Kareth was dumbfounded, but she was also fascinated. "No no else has ever seen them? Not ever?"

"Not that I know of." He finished his drink and set the can beside his chair as he propped his feet on the railing.

"Lake Thorsen," she proclaimed, "hang on to your hat because you're about to be discovered on 'Texas Lifestyles.'" Her voice was full of excitement and her mind was already planning the interview.

2

No, I'm not," his voice answered in the darkness.

Kareth gave him an encouraging smile. "Trust me. You'll be a marvelous success on my program. As far as I know, there isn't another wood sculptor in this area, certainly not one who does life-size figures. Even if the network doesn't pick it up, you'll be locally famous overnight."

"I don't want to be discovered."

Kareth peered at him through the night. Illuminated as he was by the porch light, she couldn't make out his features. Was he serious? "You don't?"

"No. I don't." His deep voice was quiet but firm.

"That seems like a rather irresponsible attitude to me."

"Why does it matter to you one way or another?

Up until a couple of hours ago you'd never heard of me."

"It's not for you personally," she hedged. If the sculptor had been less attractively packaged, would she still be so insistent? she briefly wondered, then dismissed the thought. "I was only thinking of your art. You don't have to decide now. I've made the offer. Think it over and let me know later."

In the ensuing silence the peaceful night sounds of the country emerged from the deep woods. Crickets and katydids chorused against the deeper note of the owl. No sounds of traffic reached the house and to Kareth's city-bred ears, this seemed strange indeed. Overhead the Milky Way dusted the velvet sky in an unfathomable arch.

"Have you lived here long?" Lake asked. "I haven't seen you around town."

"I moved here last year."

"How did you happen to pick Livingston?"

"The television station manager saw me working as a reporter in Los Angeles and he offered me a show. I travel around the area looking for interesting people to interview. I guess you'd say it's similar to the 'Eyes of Texas' show, only on a more local scale."

"You were on television in California? Not the movies? I thought that was the big dream."

"It is," she said wryly. "However, not everyone makes it. I nearly did though. I had a part in a grade B movie—I even had a line. I shinnied up a pole and tied a Hawaiian shirt to it as a flag and said, 'Let's get on with the party!' When none of the major studios snapped me up, I decided to face reality. I could continue doing bit parts in such classy movies as *Surfing Bingo* or I could turn to TV. I chose the latter. I saw too many people just growing old waiting for a big break."

"*Surfing Bingo?*" Lake laughed.

"It was all its name promised and more." She grinned. "Even I wasn't that starstruck."

"So why Livingston?" he prompted. "Why didn't you stay in L.A.?"

"They had an opening here, so I came to town to look things over and be looked over by the boss. He liked me and I loved the area, so I stayed. I've been happy with my decision ever since. Especially at five o'clock when I used to spend two hours snarled in a colossal traffic jam."

"I know what you mean. Houston has one just like it." Before she could ask if he had lived there, he said, "So that's why it's so important to 'discover' me? Because you climbed that flagpole and no one cheered?"

Kareth riveted her eyes on the darkness beyond the porch rail. "You have a very unsettling way of cutting through to the heart of things." She tossed him a challenging glare. "I guess that's part of it. So what? I'm also damned good at what I do and my show has a high rating."

This time his voice was gentle and almost caressing. "I wasn't trying to make you mad. My guess is that you're good at everything you set your mind to."

Kareth had no answer for this. His previous observation had been far too accurate for comfort. In her depressed moments she saw herself as a cross between Diogenes and Arthur Godfrey—searching the hills and valleys for a person with talent that she could boost to the top. In her saner moments she knew she was the popular emcee of a well-received show. But always she knew she had not quite achieved what she'd set out to do.

When Lake spoke she jumped. He had been so quiet, she had almost forgotten he was there. "If I had been there to see you climb that pole, I would have cheered."

A smile tilted her lips. "I'm not so sure I'd like being a movie star. Not anymore. Watching the years creep up and knowing the best parts were written for women younger and more beautiful. I'm twenty-eight. Before long I'd be cast in 'character' roles or as someone's mother."

"You aren't exactly over the hill. As for a woman more beautiful, that's hard to imagine."

"Don't!" she said sharply. "Don't play the gallant with me. Expecially when I'm being so painfully honest with you."

"You misunderstood. I'm an artist and I was commenting on your beauty in a purely professional way. You *are* lovely."

"Oh."

"And if you believe that's all I meant, I've got a bridge you may want to buy."

Kareth tried to pierce the shadows to see his face but gave up. "If you don't mind, I think I'll go to bed now."

"Sure thing." Lake uncoiled his long frame from the porch chair and waited for her to precede him into the house.

Kareth walked self-consciously, all too aware of his eyes upon her back. Again she wondered if she had been foolish to accept his offer of a place to spend the night. Still, it was too late to change her mind and she didn't really want to stay alone in the near-solid darkness. She followed his gesture and mounted the stairs. At the top she turned and tilted her head questioningly.

"In here." He pushed open the door to the right and stepped aside for her to enter.

The room was done in delft blue and white. Crisp curtains hung at the windows and a needlepoint rug covered most of the floor. A maple rocker with a blue cushion sat in one corner and the walls sported bright watercolors that bore the signature "Thorsen."

"It was my parents' room," Lake explained. "I use it for guests. There are clean sheets on the bed and the bathroom is through that door. If you need anything, you can look for it yourself or call me— whichever you prefer."

Kareth looked up into his moss green eyes. He was studying her as if her every movement intrigued him. His expressive lips held a faint smile and his strong hands were hooked in the back pockets of his jeans. His soft blue sweatshirt made her hands long to touch him.

"I won't need anything," she managed to say. "Once I lie down I don't even turn over until morning." This made her sound too vulnerable, so she added, "At least that's true at home. In a strange place I'm very alert."

The grin was spreading across his face as he listened to her stick both feet in her mouth at once.

"There *is* a lock, isn't there?" she demanded suspiciously.

With an extravagant gesture he indicated the doorknob. "I'd offer you pajamas, but I don't own any. There may be a robe in the closet. Sometimes a friend leaves something behind."

Kareth nodded. He didn't own any pajamas. Only the sight of the old-fashioned silver lock beneath the glass doorknob gave her a measure of security.

Lake knew he ought to go. Reason told him he should have merely opened the door for her and left. But his feet seemed rooted to the rug. In the lamplight her hair was the color of dark honey—too deep for blond and too light to be called brown. Highlights, almost reddish in hue, gleamed in the thick waves and he knew that if he touched those tresses, they would be soft and fragrant. Her eyes were the color of a pond on a cloudy day. Intelligence shone there and a sense of humor lurked nearby. He was sure of that by the way her lips tilted up even when she wasn't laughing.

Somehow, without really willing it, he stepped closer to her. He could see a pulse racing in the hollow of her throat and he reached out to put his fingertips beside it. Her skin was warm and creamy, just as he had thought it would be. He hesitated and when she didn't draw back, he bent his head and slowly claimed her lips.

Her breath was sweet in his mouth and her lips parted willingly. Slowly her small hands traveled up his arms to rest upon his chest and he wondered if she could feel the thunder of his heart.

For a long moment he drank of her sweetness, then his arms encircled her and he drew her close. Her arms drifted about his neck and he ran his fingers through her mane of hair. The strands were silken and he was pleased to note that she didn't use hair spray. As naturally as a flower turns to the sun, her head tilted back. She kissed him longingly and her lithe body flowed against his.

With a great effort Lake pulled away, steadying her when she swayed toward him. Her eyes were the intense gray of a stormy sky and her lips were still slightly parted from his kiss. Lake felt a muscle tighten in his temple from the effort it had taken to release her. He wasn't at all sure what had happened in those brief moments. Whatever it was had been building ever since she'd stepped out into the clearing a few hours before. He had been half afraid to speak then for fear of scaring her away, and now he was aware of the same sensation.

A look of bewilderment came into her eyes as if she, too, were deeply touched by whatever had just happened. Lake felt his body quicken and he stepped back. Whatever this feeling was, it was still too fragile. He felt it and he knew she did, too.

Using all his will power, he smoothed her hair back from her face and smiled. "Good night," he said gently. "I'll see you in the morning."

Kareth stared after him in shock. What had happened? Had he possibly felt the spark that had leaped to life within her? Somehow she managed to murmur, "Good night."

Unable to move, she watched him turn and walk away, then pull the door shut behind him. A part of her seemed to go with him. As if in a dream, she lifted her fingertips to her lips still soft and moist from his kiss. She had heard of love at first sight. She had even scoffed about it at parties and said she would believe it when she saw it. Now she did.

Slowly she went to the door and leaned her forehead against the cool wood. All this was a dream, she told herself. Tomorrow in the clear light of day she would feel foolish for having let him kiss her, much less for thinking it was more than a casual gesture. But tonight her senses were reeling and her thoughts fluttered like trapped birds.

With numb fingers she turned the silver lock—not because she feared him, but because she somehow feared herself. She knew it would be a long night.

She was right. The hours dragged by. She tossed and turned until she was exhausted and the sheets had pulled loose from the foot of the bed. Somewhere nearby he lay sleeping. He might live a lonely life, but that kiss had been anything but unpracticed. No doubt he was the sort of man who kissed as casually as some shake hands. The thought didn't help. Whatever he was or did, Kareth wasn't that sort at all. She didn't rush into things. It just wasn't her nature.

Pulling the pillow over her head, with her feet hanging off the side of the bed, Kareth finally found sleep. Her dreams were far from restful, dealing as they did with golden Vikings and magic unicorns, but when she awoke she was smiling.

Light streamed in through the curtains and she could hear the trill of a mockingbird in the big oak. She couldn't have had more than a few hours sleep, but she felt keenly alive down to her toes.

On bare feet she padded into the adjoining bathroom to make herself ready to begin the day. She applied what little makeup she had in her purse and was pleased with the results. Since she had to wear quite a bit of makeup under the bright television lights, she preferred to use a bare minimum off camera. As she brushed her long hair, it fell into the gleaming, natural waves that she had viewed as a curse when she was a child. Humming under her breath, she went back into the bedroom and quickly dressed. Like Lake, she didn't wear night clothes either, and hadn't missed them.

Still humming, she went to the door and pulled it open.

Her song died abruptly as she realized she had not turned the lock at all. She shut the door, twisted the lever and opened it again. The lock was broken!

Feeling definitely miffed, she went downstairs in search of Lake. She found him in the kitchen, frying bacon. "The lock on that door doesn't work!" she accused.

"I know. It never has." He grinned at her. "Good morning."

"Then why did you tell me it did!"

"I never said any such thing. You asked if there was a lock and I said there was, which was the truth."

"But you knew what I meant!"

"I didn't come in, did I? The lock worked."

Feeling oddly deflated, she had to nod. He had known her door was unlocked and hadn't even tried to open it.

As if he could hear her thoughts, he said, "Unless I'm invited in, I keep my distance. Molesting women isn't my hobby." He added, "I hope you like scrambled eggs, because the yolks just broke."

"Scrambled is fine." As if she had done this every day of her life, Kareth took a cup from the rack and poured herself some coffee. Why had he stopped with only a kiss last night? He was either completely unimpressed by her, or he was the most honorable man she had ever met. She watched him over the rim of the coffee cup. He had scarcely glanced at her.

"That lock was a family joke of sorts," Lake explained. "My father was no good at fixing anything. Mom did all the repairs and was even pretty good at keeping the car running. One day Dad decided to surprise her by putting a lock on the bedroom door. We never did figure out what he did to it, but it never once worked. Mom refused to fix it because she was touched by his effort. They had a good relationship."

"What happened to them?"

"A car wreck. They both died at the scene. It was pretty hard on me at the time, but I can't imagine one without the other. That's the way they would have chosen, I expect."

Kareth sat in silence for a while. She had never known a couple like that and in a way she envied their closeness. Abruptly she asked, "Were you ever married?"

"Yes, for five years. I met her in college and we lived in Houston."

"You divorced her?"

"It was mutual. Thinking back, the divorce was the only thing we ever did agree upon. It was a case of opposites that attracted and then spent the next five years repelling."

"Where is she now?"

"Still in Houston as far as I know. If we had wanted to stay in touch, we wouldn't have gotten divorced." He glanced over at her. "What about you?"

"I've never married. First I was too busy to settle down and then I couldn't find any one person that I wanted to see every day for the rest of my life." She paused, then added, "While I was in California I lived with a man. Neither of us wanted to get married because we had heard of too many divorces and we wanted to see if it would last. It didn't and when we split up, it was as bad as I've always imagined a divorce would be. Funny, isn't it?"

"No. Were you hurt?"

She shrugged. "Does it matter? I know now that it was the best thing that could have come of the relationship."

Lake's eyes met hers with a depth of understanding that made her smile wryly and add, "Yes, I was hurt."

He scooped half the eggs onto her plate along with some bacon and biscuits and put both plates on the table. "These are canned biscuits—an old family recipe."

Kareth smiled. "One of your mother's?"

"Nope, Dad's. Mom didn't like to cook."

When they finished, Lake washed the dishes as Kareth dried. She found him easy to be with and although she had confided much more to him than she would have to anyone other than Peg, she felt perfectly at ease. This, she realized with a start, was trust. A commodity she was normally lacking.

With the last dish put away, Lake led Kareth out the back door and took a deep breath of air. "Isn't that great? If they could grow air like this in a city, it would be worth a fortune."

She matched her steps to his as he wandered across the backyard. Several out-buildings flanked the house, but he guided her past them and into the field. Vivid bluebonnets carpeted the undulating pasture, interspersed with Indian paintbrushes and buttercups of pale pink with dusty yellow centers.

Again Kareth had the sensation of being in a dream world. During the long night she had almost convinced herself that this tranquility hadn't really existed. Now she glanced at Lake, his pale hair blowing in the wind and his eyes reflecting the verdant field, and she wondered if her imagination had done justice to her surroundings.

They strolled through knee-high flowers that buzzed with honeybees. Butterflies skipped like wind-tossed flowers and a covey of quail broke cover almost under their feet. Kareth jumped, then watched with interest as the plump brown bodies fluttered to a new hiding place.

"It's all alive out here," Lake said contentedly. "Every inch of it."

Somehow, coming from him and in this place, the words sounded as natural as rainfall. A smile tugged at her lips.

"You know," he said without looking at her, "you look better without makeup than any woman I ever saw." Almost in the same breath he pointed at the woods and said, "I have a shed over there and we can get a gas can to give your car a transfusion."

At his unexpected compliment Kareth had nearly stumbled. She had been positive he hadn't really looked at her once all morning. He held out his hand to steady her and a tingle raced up her arm at his touch. She caught her breath and their eyes met—hers startled and confused, his thoughtful. Hastily she let go of his hand.

Lake went to a shed half hidden by tall haw bushes and took out a square can of gasoline. Kareth looked around the interior at the various saws and winches he obviously used in his sculpting. He was avoiding her eyes and she felt a wave of confusion. Had she done something wrong? Maybe he had felt nothing at their touch and she was merely being foolish.

They left the shed and Lake led her to the path they had taken the night before. Soon she heard the song of the creek as it splashed over the roots and mini-waterfalls in its race to join the river. Seen in the daylight, the bridge melted naturally into its surroundings. The rough cedar rail felt damp under her hand and the water coursed several feet beneath the wide planks.

As before, she was startled by the appearance of the bridge troll. His knotty face was grimacing in a mean little grin beneath a sock-shaped cap that was carved onto his head. One hand presented the dragon.

The mythical beast coiled in fierce undulations around red bud trees, its scaly feet resting solidly on the ground, its proud head reared back to breathe flame on any trespasser. The mottled, shifting shade of the leaves seemed to make the scales shimmer and ripple.

"How magnificent!" Kareth breathed. "How do you make them so lifelike?"

Lake shrugged. "Wood is alive. This particular tree was blown down by a tornado a couple of years ago. It was a white oak, with branches that twisted every which way. The more I looked at it, the more I saw the dragon. After that, it was only a matter of carving away everything that wasn't dragon."

Kareth's eyes were full of respect. "I think you really *are* a genius."

They left the bridge and went to the dragon. Kareth ran her hand over the scales, some warmed to near-life by the sun, others cooled to earth moistness.

"I don't understand," she said at last. "All these masterpieces out here in the open. Aren't you afraid someone will steal them?"

Lake laughed. "Do you have any idea what that dragon weighs? Anybody big enough to carry it off is welcome to it."

"No, really. What about the small ones, like the troll or the fairies? They could be stolen."

"No, they can't. They belong here. If something belongs to a place, it won't be taken away."

She frowned. "That's not logical. Things are stolen every day."

He grinned obstinately. "Not these."

Still unconvinced, Kareth walked back to the path. She wasn't about to agree with his odd theory. "I guess you are pretty much out of the way here. That's a safety factor."

"Have it your own way." He held aside a sweet-gum limb so she could pass. "Are you going to work today?"

"I'm off on Saturday. I had hoped to find the woman I was looking for and set up an interview. She's a midwife who has been working this area for fifty years. I don't suppose you know of her?"

"Ma Dyer? Sure I do. She delivered me, as a matter of fact." He nodded at Kareth's amazed expression. "I told you my parents were rather eccentric. She lives down the dirt road you're parked on. It's only three or four miles."

"Why didn't you tell me that last night? I could have borrowed your gas, done my interview, and gone home."

He regarded her in a thoughtful manner. "Would you have preferred that?"

Kareth found herself shaking her head. When he

looked deep into her eyes like that, she couldn't lie. "No, I wouldn't."

He smiled. "Besides, you would have gotten hopelessly lost between here and the main road."

She frowned. "There's one thing I don't understand. How do you get to town? No car could drive down this path."

Without meeting her eyes he said, "I take the other road."

"What road!"

"The one just beyond the barn. It's a straight shot to the highway."

"Then why . . . !" she sputtered.

"Because your car is over on the back road. As you pointed out, you couldn't drive it up this path. You have to wind back the way you came to get to the highway from there. Don't worry, I'll draw you a map."

Kareth tried to glare at him. He might not have lied, but he had certainly omitted a great deal.

"I'll also mark the more direct route to my house. It's much easier to find from the other direction."

"What makes you think I'll be back?" she countered.

"I'm hoping you will." Unexpectedly he caught her arm and pulled her to him. Weaving his fingers through her hair, he kissed her thoroughly, gently.

Kareth felt the ground rock and she held to him tightly as her mind reeled. Beneath his pullover shirt his body was hard and sinewy without a spare ounce of flesh. Her breasts pressed against him and her body matched itself to his. His tongue caressed the soft moistness of her inner lips and traced the tiny ridges of her teeth as fireworks sparked and showered all through her.

When he finally released her, she kept her hands on his taut biceps to steady herself. She seemed drawn toward him as if he were a lodestone.

"Please come back," he said huskily.

"I will," she promised.

"When?" He wasn't going to let her slip away without a firm agreement.

"Monday," she managed to say. The sun was glinting in his eyes and robbing her of all thought. "I have an interview to shoot not far from here." That wasn't entirely true, but she would be within fifty miles.

He smiled and her heart rocked. "I'll be expecting you."

"I didn't say what time," she reminded him.

"I'll be looking for you from now until you show up."

"Before five o'clock," she murmured dreamily. "I'll be here before five."

Earnestness filled his eyes as he cupped her face tenderly. "Don't get lost, honey. But if you do, just sit tight and I'll find you."

"You know," she whispered, "I think you mean that."

"I do. I've searched for you for a long time. Now

that I know what you look like, it'll be much easier to find you again.''

Kareth's lips were parted with wonder at the magic of his words but she dared not question him. Those were words to dream on, to ponder, not to explain until they became prosaic and normal.

She seemed to float the rest of the way to her car. True to his word, Lake drew her a map on the back of a business letter. On her state map he pointed out the turns and circled the location of his farm. Kareth listened to his words, but a great deal of her attention was focused on the way laugh lines fanned out at the corners of his eyes when he became engrossed in the map and how the tendons flowed in his thick forearms as he sketched in the road and landmarks.

He fueled her car from the can and assured her she could reach the nearest gas station with no difficulty. It was time to go. There were no more words and all the actions had been accomplished. Kareth gazed up at him and tried to think of some reason to stay. He seemed to be having the same mental struggle.

Finally Kareth held out her hand. Lake took it, not in a handshake, but in an endearing caress. Their eyes met and spoke far more than their lips could do as yet.

"Monday," he said at last.

Kareth nodded and got into her car. She turned the key and the engine purred to life. No hope of delaying there. She smiled up at him and drove away. In her rearview mirror she could still see him standing in the road, watching her. Only after she was well on her way to the midwife's house did she realize she had forgotten to call Peg and tell her not to worry.

3

Kareth, beside her cameraman, mounted the wooden porch and pressed the small round buzzer. From deep in the farmhouse she heard the responding summons. She gazed across the narrow yard edged with pinks and day lilies to where a flock of white turkeys returned her perusal.

Heavy clouds banked the trees in mounds like shaving cream and a humid stillness promised rain by nightfall. "Will we have enough light to shoot, Charley?" she asked her companion.

He shifted the weighty camera to his other hand and nodded. "This shouldn't take that long."

Kareth glanced at her watch. She certainly hoped it wouldn't. She had promised Lake that she'd be there by five and that seemed infinitely more important than the interview she was about to conduct. Keeping her mind on her business had been very hard to do since she'd wandered upon Lake Thorsen. Had it been only two days since she had first seen him? It seemed like she'd known him forever. The sound of footsteps going from hard-wood floor to rug to wood again drew Kareth's eyes back to the door.

"Why, hello." The plump woman greeted Kareth and Charley as if their arrival was indeed a surprise. "Come in, come in." The woman was dressed resplendently in a flowered silk dress and was sur-rounded by the scent of her powder and perfume. Her fastidiously curled hair spoke of hours at a beauty shop and her aging lips were painted vermil-ion. "Harold? They're here," she announced.

Harold Dupree entered on his cue and held out his hand to Kareth. Like his wife, Harold was dressed to the teeth. He stood uncomfortably in his shiny black suit, and his narrow red-striped tie seemed to threat-en to pinch his head from his shoulders. His thinning dark hair lay slicked close to his head and his normally red face was scrubbed to an even rosier hue.

"Mr. Dupree," Kareth protested, "I asked you to dress casually. Don't you remember?"

He grinned and made a sideways gesture with his head. His wife tittered, causing her stomach to quiver with mirth. "Go on with you. Harold couldn't appear on television wearing old clothes."

"But Mrs. Dupree, we wanted him to look as if we just dropped by unexpectedly," Kareth tried to explain. "We wanted to see him at work."

"Call me Mavis," the woman urged. "Harold can show you around in his good clothes." She chuckled conspiratorially. "I never could stand those old overalls of his."

"I rather liked them," Kareth argued. "And that housedress you wore when I was out here before. It was very becoming."

"That old thing? For television?" She tried to shoo Kareth and Charley into the parlor. "I made coffee and a pound cake. Have a seat while I get it."

"Kareth, we really need to shoot while the light is good," Charley protested.

"He's right, Mrs. Dupree. There's a storm brewing."

"What storm? Maybe a little rain, but it doesn't look like much. And please call me Mavis."

"Nevertheless, we really do need to start. Mr. Dupree, will you come outside?"

"Harold," his wife prompted. Harold merely grinned self-consciously.

Kareth preceded the others out and pointed toward the largest pen. "Let's set up there, Charley. I want the coop in the background."

"You got it." He carried the Minicam to the spot she had indicated.

"Now, Mr. Dupree, this will be very simple. I want

us to just talk. I'll ask questions and you answer me in your own words. Okay?"

Harold grinned and nodded.

"You aren't nervous, are you?" She knew he could speak. She had talked to him herself.

"He is a little," his wife chimed in helpfully. "See, we've never been on television before."

"There's nothing to be nervous about," Kareth reassured them. "It's taped, not live, so if you make a mistake, it doesn't matter. Just be yourselves." She noticed Mavis was wearing frosted eye shadow that in the sunlight seemed to glow. "Charley, let's keep the camera back for full-length shots. Maybe a little wide-angle, too." This way the eye shadow wouldn't be as glaring and the turkeys would be clearly visible throughout the segment.

She positioned the couple by the wire mesh gate and went to look through the camera lens. Harold and Mavis stood in frozen stances, set smiles pasted on their faces. Kareth gave them an easygoing grin to loosen them up as she joined them.

"I understand you've been raising albino turkeys for some time now," she said conversationally as the camera spun silently.

"Are we on?" Mavis asked in a stage whisper.

"Cut, Charley." Kareth smiled at the woman. "Please, Mrs. Dupree, just ignore Charley. Forget he's here."

"Call me Mavis. All right." To Charley she said, "Roll 'em."

Kareth continued to smile but her lips were beginning to feel stiff. "I understand you've been raising albino turkeys for some time, Mr. Dupree?"

"Harold," corrected Mavis.

"Hold it, Kareth. The turkeys are gone," Charley called out.

Kareth looked over at the pen. All the big birds were clustered near Charley, peering and gobbling softly at the sight of something they hadn't seen before.

"Ain't nothing as curious as a turkey." Harold spoke up at last. "I've seen 'em climb up on top of each other to watch Mavis hang out a wash."

"Really?" Kareth said encouragingly as Charley swung around to film the turkeys in a close-up.

"Go on with you. Hang out the wash indeed," Mavis objected. "You know I have a new dryer."

Harold, emboldened by his verbal foray, grinned and nodded at Kareth. "She does for a fact. Old man Kessler installed it last week. He does right good work. If you want a washer or a dryer, you ought to go to him."

"I'll remember that," Kareth said smoothly. So far most of this taping would be unusable. "Tell me about these turkeys. What do they weigh?"

"Oh, that big one there might weigh—"

"Harold, that's not the biggest one. That one over there looks bigger to me," Mavis interrupted.

"Does it now? Well, I believe you may be right.

No, that's a bigger one there on the back side of the flock. Point your camera over there, boy. See if you can't find that one by the hen with the pecked head."

Kareth managed not to groan. Some interviews went more smoothly than others.

"Harold, go pick up that young one there," Mavis instructed. To Kareth and the camera she said, "I have it marked for our dinner next Thanksgiving. I have a recipe for dressing that uses two cups of cooked cornbread. . . . Not that one, Harold, the other one. A cup of bread crumbs . . ."

Kareth suspected this interview was going to be more difficult than most. She risked a glance at her watch and grimaced.

Two hours later she finally waved farewell to the Duprees. She backed out of the drive and followed Charley's car down the black-topped road. Although her windows were closed and her air-conditioner was on, the unpleasant odor of the turkey farm seemed to still be with her. Cautiously she sniffed her palm. The smell caused her to wrinkle her nose.

Charley turned back toward town but she continued on down the road, Lake's map on the seat beside her. She was later than she had expected to be, but who could have guessed that the open, helpful Duprees would have been so difficult to interview? She would have enough tape for the show, but she dreaded having to edit it. By the time she cut out Mavis's recipes and all the anecdotes about the grandchildren, there would scarcely be more than the five minutes she needed.

She turned down the farm-to-market road and let the miles flow beneath her car. Surely, she decided for the hundredth time, Lake wasn't as intriguing as her memory portrayed him. For the past two days he had rarely been out of her thoughts. She was looking forward to this evening as an exorcism of sorts. Once she saw him again she could put everything in perspective. Perhaps she would date him, perhaps not. In any event, she was sure he would prove to be a very normal man and not the Viking enchanter she remembered.

She grimaced wryly. In her thoughts she had painted him bigger than life, with a sensuous mystique no man could really have. At one point she had even wondered if she loved him! Kareth let out a derisive laugh. It made her feel more in control, so she did it again.

Lake's directions were simple and easy to follow, and she soon caught sight of his two-story house and its flanking barn and out-buildings. She slowed, almost regretting that she had returned. He had become nearly legendary in her thoughts and dreams. Now she would see him again in the light of day, in ordinary surroundings, and the luster would fade and vanish. Kareth had always prided herself on being level-headed and down to earth.

She turned onto the drive that curved up to his

lawn and parked beneath the sheltering oak. The sky was leaden and solid-looking, making the cabin seem like a secure haven against the coming storm.

Kareth got out but before she could close her car door, the front door opened and Lake stepped out onto the porch.

He must have heard her drive up, she told herself. He might even have seen her from a distance and waited for her to park before coming to greet her. But her mind rejected those rational explanations. It was as if he had known when to step out from some sixth sense that had tuned him to her and her alone. It was the same sense that made her want to run to him and fling herself into his arms and let the world spin on without her.

"I'm late," she said without moving.

"I don't own a watch." He stepped forward and stopped as if he, too, were trying to rationalize the situation.

"The interview took longer than I expected." She realized with a start that he was even more handsome and virile than she had remembered. He wore dark jeans and a cotton knit pullover the shade of mushrooms. In spite of his casual attire, he had an almost royal air about him, a natural elegance.

"Are you going to stay out there? Should I come to you?" he teased softly. "Maybe we could meet halfway."

Feeling foolish, Kareth slammed her car door and walked briskly up the flat stone walk. She was letting her imagination run away with her again. Who had ever seen a Viking in blue jeans and Topsiders?

When she reached him, Lake lifted his hand toward her hair as if to caress it. Kareth stopped and her eyes met his as electricity crackled between them. Slowly he lowered his hand and held out a white feather on his palm.

"Yours?" he asked in his deeply mellow voice.

Kareth laughed and took the feather to twirl it between her thumb and forefinger. "A memento from the Duprees' Thanksgiving turkey. They let me hold it." She blew on the feather, sending it floating down the steps. "I never realized how heavy turkeys are. Nor how aromatic. May I wash my hands? I've never seen so many turkeys in my life. If one moved, they all followed the one in front. An airplane flew over and they went crazy." She was babbling and she knew it, but his presence was unnerving in the extreme. "Mr. and Mrs. Dupree wore their best clothes in spite of my saying I wanted them to look the way they do around the house on a usual day. Not that they didn't look nice, but Mr. Dupree's black suit looked pretty odd in the turkey pen."

Lake put his forefinger under her chin and tilted her head up. Before she knew what was happening, he was kissing her.

Kareth's memory had indeed been faulty. His kiss swept her away to castles in billowing clouds and promised loving such as she had never known before. When he finally lifted his head, she gazed dreamily up into his unfathomable eyes. Then she let her arms glide up and pull him back down to kiss her again.

His lips were soft yet firm as they met hers and Kareth felt her own open willingly to his questing tongue. A deep wonder flooded through her as Lake's arms tightened. His embrace was more than just exciting—it was protective. Loving. Right. A small moan escaped Kareth's throat and she felt an answering tremor run through him.

This time when he pulled away she could read the confused longing in the mossy depths of his eyes. He gazed down at her as silence spun around them. A small muscle tightened in his jaw as he ran his thumb along the firm line of her chin.

"Kareth," he murmured. "I had told myself you weren't real. That no woman could just wander out of the woods and make me feel like this. I was wrong. You kiss me and something explodes inside me. If it didn't feel so good, lady, I'd say you were danger-ous." He tried to laugh, but the sound died as he looked down at her with a perplexed expression.

"Lake," she whispered, making his name an endearment, "what's happening to us?"

"Damned if I know," he replied quietly. Abruptly he stepped back and ran his fingers through his hair before hooking his thumbs in the back pockets of his jeans. "Let's go for a walk."

"Now?" she said in surprise. Her world felt disjointed and spun of dreamdust and he wanted to go for a walk? "It's getting ready to rain."

"Haven't you ever walked in the rain? Come on."

She glanced down at her clothes. Her blouse was a cotton and synthetic blend, as were her slacks, and water wouldn't hurt her low-heeled shoes. With a shrug she followed him down the porch steps.

Lake walked briskly, as if he were trying to put distance between himself and whatever had just flared into being on the porch. Kareth had to hurry to keep up, even though her long legs were usually a match for anybody. She, too, felt ambivalent about whatever it was that their kisses unleashed. This was no time for her to get involved. Not with her show still commanding so much of her attention. Especially not with a man who lived in the Big Thicket and carved fantasies from tree trunks. Kareth had never been a social climber, but she had also never pictured herself in a log cabin surrounded by a nearly impenetrable forest.

After a while their steps slowed and Kareth risked a glance at Lake. "Maybe I ought to leave," she said half-heartedly. "Cut this off now. While we can."

"Do you want that?" he asked with studied casualness as he held aside a branch.

Kareth walked by him on the path for several yards before she answered. "No. I don't want to leave you."

He nodded. "I think it was too late the first time we saw each other."

"Don't say that. Do you know how scary that is to me?"

"I didn't mean to scare you."

She walked a little farther before she said cautiously, "I'm not afraid of you. I'm afraid of how I feel every time you kiss me—or even just look at me."

"Don't be afraid, Kareth," he said gently. "I'll never hurt you. Not on purpose."

Their footfalls were barely audible on the forest's spongy carpet. Somewhere a bird called out a single repetitive note. In the far distance thunder rolled with a velvet voice.

"Where are we going?" Kareth asked at last.

"To Lanewood. It's not far from here."

"I thought you said it's not there anymore."

"Technically it's not. All the people have moved away and it's a ghost town now. My parents bought the land it sits on and had planned to convert it into a tourist attraction, furnish it as it had been back in the thirties when it was built. That was during the big oil boom just north of here and many thought the oil field would extend down this far. It didn't and after a while the town folded."

"Your folks died before they could carry out their plans?"

"No, they gave them up long before that."

"Why?" She stepped over a mossy log and hurried to catch up with him.

"The tourists." He laughed. "They had overlooked the fact that a tourist attraction draws a crowd. They decided their privacy was more important."

"Oh." She looked up at him to see if he was teasing her, but he seemed to be quite serious. "That's a very . . . unusual . . . attitude."

"They were unusual people."

She thought about his refusal to exhibit his work and realized he was very much like them. Before she could ask any more questions, he swept aside a thick bush and pointed. "There it is."

Lanewood was all its name implied. The small buildings faced a single street and the woods had battled the pavement and won, so that green shoots sprouted in clumps between broken-down road rubble. The buildings were mostly built from wood, but a few were constructed of pinkish-yellow bricks shaped like a child's building blocks. Most of the windows were broken and loose tin creaked on the roofs when a breeze blew.

"What a strange place," Kareth marveled as she passed an ancient and very rusted car that had been abandoned between two buildings. She looked in the window of what had been a barbershop. It was bare except for shelves with a few broken bottles and a stained and torn barber's chair that even fifty years before hadn't been considered worth moving. "It's as if all the people just packed up and left."

"They did. It was a boom town and when the oil quit, the people moved to a more likely spot."

"But I don't see any houses," she said doubtfully.

"There were rooms above several of the stores or in storerooms behind them. Most of the people lived in tents."

"Tents?"

"Why build if you may have to move on? Few had families with them. They worked their shifts, slept, then worked again." He looked up and down the deserted street. "They were after riches or, in some cases, enough money to feed themselves and their people back home. If the field had held out, they would have stayed and built homes. It didn't. Most of them moved on to the Kilgore oil field."

Kareth walked gingerly over the boardwalk and peeped in the window of what had been the general store. "You sure know a lot about the town."

"My mother grew up not far from here. She was barely in school when the last of the people moved away, but she heard stories about the place and passed them on to me."

"It seems so eerie to be here when there isn't anyone else." She wandered over to the door and managed to shove open the warped wood. "Ever see any ghosts around here?" she asked, only half kidding.

"Just that one," Lake answered, gesturing toward the back.

For an unreasoning moment Kareth thought she *was* seeing a ghost holding a hand out toward her. Then logic returned and she saw that the "ghost" was merely another of Lake's superb carvings. She pressed her hand to her throat, where her heart fluttered wildly. "She gave me quite a turn."

"Sorry," he said with a grin. "I thought you saw it when you looked in the window." He walked over to the lady and rested his hand on her shoulder. "She was one of my first tries at sculpting a life-size figure. We had planned to carve a whole town full, dress them in real clothes, have them sort of mingle with the tourists."

"That's a marvelous idea!"

Lake wiped the dust from the chiseled features and said, "Maybe someday I'll follow through with it. I'm not as much of a hermit as my parents were."

"Think what a show it would make!" Kareth said enthusiastically. "I'll bet the network would be interested in this!"

"Not the way it is now." Lake laughed. "I'll tell you what. Someday we'll turn Lanewood into a tourist mecca. I'll carve the figures and you can handle publicity. In between counting money and making clothes for the carvings we'll plant a twelve-foot hedge all around my place to keep the tourists out."

"We'll plant Chinese holly." She laughed. "No one can climb through that!" Suddenly she realized what they were saying and her laugh broke off in mid-note.

Lake gazed at her over the mannequin's bare shoulder as dust motes swirled and floated in a weak ray of sunlight that had found its way through the clouds. After a long time he said gruffly, "We had better be getting back to the house."

As they went out onto the grassy street the first big plops of rain spattered on the sandy pavement. Lake held out his hand to her, and after a brief hesitation Kareth took it. His hand was warm and hard, his grip reassuringly firm.

They walked under the dome of hardwood trees, neither speaking, yet communicating in some more elemental way. Kareth wondered at the ease she felt with Lake. Certainly she should have been embarrassed at having lumped her future with his. Yet she felt no uneasiness at all, now that the initial surprise had passed.

The rain peppered the leaves above and misted down in silver veils. The heady aroma of wet greenery made her draw in a deep breath. "Nothing smells as nice as a spring rain," she commented contentedly.

Lake glanced at her and seemed to relax a little. "You aren't upset at being wet?"

"Of course not. You said we were going for a walk in the rain."

"I said it, but I really thought we would be back

before it started. Otherwise I wouldn't have suggested it."

She shrugged. "I don't think I've ever walked in the rain. Oh, I guess I must have as a child, but I don't remember it. My mother would always say, 'Kareth Anne, don't you go out in the rain or you'll catch a cold.'" She laughed up at him. "She never has accepted that germs and raindrops aren't synonymous."

He grinned at her. "You really aren't upset at getting wet, are you? I like that. A lot of women would be having a fit by now."

"I can promise you I rarely have a 'fit,'" she guaranteed solemnly. "An occasional rage, maybe a tantrum, but that's about it."

"Since you didn't grow up here, I guess East Texas idioms are like a new language to you, aren't they?"

"To some extent." She smiled. "It took me a while to learn that 'fixing to go someplace' is the same thing as 'getting ready to leave.' But I love it here—the easy pace, the friendly people. It's not like anyplace I've ever lived before."

"East Texas is a place unto itself. There's nothing else quite like it. That's why I came back here."

"What did you do in Houston?" she asked.

A clap of thunder made her flinch, then laugh, her question forgotten.

"Come on," Lake said as he grabbed her hand. "If we run, we can get home before the storm hits in force."

Kareth ran beside him, their long legs racing the wind. As if the heavens detected their escape attempt, the skies opened up and a deluge of rain poured down upon them. They hurried across the drenched wildflowers in the yard and stumbled, gasping, onto the welcoming porch.

Lake caught Kareth in his arms and spun her around as the storm crashed overhead. Then he let her slide down his body until her feet touched the porch. Awestruck at his emotions, he gazed down at her dewy face and bent to kiss a raindrop off her long lashes.

"You're some woman," he said huskily. "You know that?" Gently he stroked her cheek. "I'll find you some dry clothes. By the way, I sure hope you like spaghetti, because that's what we're having for supper."

"I adore spaghetti," she whispered.

"Good," he said. "You can help me cook it." He propelled her inside and up the stairs in search of dry clothing.

4

~~~~~~~~~~

After supper Kareth washed the dishes and Lake dried them and put them away. Outside, the gentle patter of rain could be heard in the velvety darkness. In contrast, the kitchen was a haven of coziness. Kareth wiped the tile counter clean and draped the towel over a porcelain hook.

"All done," she said, "and my compliments to the chefs."

"We turn out a mean bowl of spaghetti," he agreed smugly. "We should do this on a regular basis."

Kareth smiled and tightened the belt of the voluminous terry robe she wore. She could still hear the purr of the dryer tumbling the wetness from her clothes. As if she did this nightly, she took Lake's hand and wandered barefoot with him to the den.

Plopping down on the overstuffed couch, she curled so that her head rested on the back cushion. He had built a fire to ward off the night's chill and from time to time the wind puffed aromatic wood smoke back down the chimney. He would tape so well, she thought as she watched him. His features seemed to have been sculpted for a television camera. Again she wondered how she could convince him to be on her show. To let such talent go unnoticed was too wasteful for her to consider. Perhaps, she mused, she could talk him into a small, informal showing of his work. She was positive he would be well received and his success would probably encourage him to exhibit more widely.

Lake added a log to the fire and sat beside her, slouching comfortably into the same position she had taken. "It's not the greatest fireplace in the world," he commented as the wind sent more smoke into the room. "The man that built it was getting old and I guess he did something wrong. It doesn't draw very well."

"I don't mind," she answered lazily. "I never knew anyone who built fireplaces. Think he would like to be on my show?"

"He died last spring."

She sat in contented quietness for a while. Then said, "Lake, have you thought about being on my show?"

"Not a whole lot," he drawled.

She rolled her head to look at him. "I wish you would. Not only because I have a slot to fill, but because I know you would be a success."

"I've never been on television. I wouldn't know what to say," he replied. "Not everyone feels at home in front of a camera."

"I could put you at ease." Hope leaped in her voice. "All you have to do is be yourself. Anybody can do that."

He chuckled softly. "That's easy for you to say. I would probably drive a chisel through my hand."

"Or then again, you might enjoy it," she countered. "And you might get commissions for more carvings."

"What makes you so sure I'm looking for work? I like to take my time and do things at my own pace. Besides, my sculptures are planned for this environment. Taken away they wouldn't be the same."

"I disagree. That dragon would be a masterpiece no matter where it was."

"You're wrong." He took her hand and softened his words by gently stroking her curling fingers. "I use only trees that need to be cut. My woods are in good shape now and I don't want to bring down a perfectly good tree just to carve it for a stranger."

"If you won't be on television, will you do something else for me?"

"Maybe."

"A park is being built on the far side of town. The dedication ceremony is next Wednesday. Will you exhibit one of your statues—only on loan, mind you—for the opening ceremonies?"

"Why do you want me to do that?"

"I think your creations are wonderful and I want other people to see them and appreciate your work as I do. That's not asking so much, is it?" The idea had occurred to Kareth during the wee hours that morning when she couldn't sleep for the thought of Lake and his carvings.

He studied her fingers as he ran his thumb over her shell-pink nails. "This would make you happy?"

"Yes, it would."

"Only on loan?"

"Absolutely."

With a sigh he enfolded her hand in his and met her eyes. "It's against my better judgment, but all right. I have a seven-foot Merlin in the woods behind the barn. If you can figure a way to get it to the park and back, I'll let you show it for a month."

Her eyes shining, Kareth sat up with a burst of enthusiasm and squeezed his hand. "Thank you, Lake! I'll take care of everything."

"Don't you want to see Merlin first to be sure it's appropriate?"

"There's no need for that. I've seen a lot of your work around here and it's all marvelous. I'll start making inquiries tomorrow about movers and I'll contact the mayor for permission. This is wonderful! And don't worry about Merlin. I'll make sure they take good care of him. You won't be sorry."

"I already am," he said so softly she didn't hear him.

"I can picture it now in a certain grove of pin oaks. It will look as mystical there as it does here."

"How do you know it's mystical?" he asked.

"All Merlins are. It's their birthright."

He chuckled at her excitement. "I imagine even Merlin had his pedestrian moments. Maybe I portrayed one of those."

"Did you?" she asked uncertainly.

"Climb back on your balloon. I'm only teasing. The Merlin is in the middle of calling down lightning and directing the wind, with his beard and cape swirling. He's exactly what you want."

"Perfect." With a smug smile Kareth leaned back onto the cushions.

Lake put his arm around her and pulled her closer so her head lay in the curve of his shoulder. Companionably they watched the small flames lick the underbelly of the log.

"Will you go somewhere with me tomorrow?" Kareth asked innocently.

"Probably. Where?"

"Meet me at the TV station at three. I have a show to tape and I'd like you to see how it's done."

"You never give up, do you?" he said with amusement.

"Rarely. This is one you'd like. I'm going out to the Pritchett farm to interview the woman who raises Clydesdale horses."

"Sounds like you enjoy your job."

"I do. I've always liked people and to me the show is more fun than work." The log popped, sending a spray of sparks up the sooty chimney. "Will you come watch?"

"Yes, but only because I want to see you. Not because I'm giving in about being on your show myself."

"Good enough," Kareth relented. She relaxed with her small victory. In time he would acquiesce. She was convinced that all artists had at least a touch of ham in their characters regardless of how eccentric or reclusive they might pretend to be.

Lake nuzzled in her silken hair. "You smell nice," he murmured into her ear. "Sort of like spring flowers."

She looked up at him and her lips parted in a faint smile. "I like being with you." Her eyes met his and she felt her soul winging to touch his in that curious way she had never noticed with another person. "Lake, how can I feel this way about you?"

"What do you mean?" He nuzzled her hair aside to rub his nose along the curve of her ear.

"Here I am wearing your bathrobe and this is only the second time I've ever seen you. By all rights I should be nervous at least. Especially with you nibbling at my ear."

"Don't you like it?"

"That's not the point."

"You feel at ease because you trust me. As for the robe, you can always take it off if it bothers you." His eyes held laughter as he gazed down at her.

"See? That's just what I mean! If any other man said that to me, I'd leave in a huff. Instead, you make me smile. It's as if I've known you forever."

"Maybe you have. What I feel for you doesn't seem like a new relationship either. Maybe we've been together in other lifetimes, other places."

"Reincarnation?" she asked doubtfully. "You believe in it?"

"Who knows for sure? I told you I had an unorthodox upbringing. At any rate, and for whatever reason, I'm more comfortable around you than I ever have been with anyone."

"Even your ex-wife?"

"Especially her."

"I never thought much about having had past lives," she mused, "but I can just imagine you as a Viking warrior on your dragon ship, skimming through the waves and pillaging the English coasts."

"And scooping up an Anglo hostage with silver eyes and hair like fresh syrup." His head dived down into the ticklish hollow of her neck.

Kareth squealed playfully and tried to wriggle away, but his powerful arms entrapped her. She tilted her head back and her eyes sparkled as she said, "Would you really have taken me hostage?"

"Damn right. But I might never have let you go."

Laughter melted from her and she saw the seriousness behind his teasing eyes. The seconds spun long as each seemed to be holding his breath in preparation for . . . what?

"I don't know how to answer you," Kareth said softly. "I keep forgetting that I really don't know you at all."

"I know," he admitted in a low voice. "I have the same trouble."

"You're so easy to be with. I can say things I wouldn't dream of saying to a casual acquaintance."

"We aren't casual acquaintances."

"Then what are we?"

Now he was silent. His eyes studied her face as if it were more precious, more worthy of remembrance than any face he had ever seen before. "I don't know what we are or what we will be. I guess that's up to us."

Kareth felt as if she were teetering on a brink. To one side was all she had ever needed or wanted; to the other lay desolation, loneliness. But she couldn't tell which side was which. "You scare the daylights out of me," she whispered.

"Lady, I was just thinking the same thing about you."

From the back of the house came a metallic buzz that signaled her clothes were ready. Starting guiltily Kareth sat up. "I . . . my clothes are dry," she stammered. "I guess I had better put them back on."

Lake reclined with a sigh against the cushions and shook his head. "I'm going to rip out that damned buzzer," he told her conversationally.

With a weak smile Kareth hurried from the room, her knees feeling like warm Jell-O. By the time she retrieved her blouse and slacks from the dryer, she was able to upbraid herself severely. What was she thinking of to let herself become so vulnerable? He was going to get an entirely false impression of her. She had not only cuddled against him like a kitten, she had actually giggled when he tickled her neck. Unforgivable! He would think she was the sort to tumble in and out of beds with no compunction at all.

She went into the downstairs bath and dressed hastily. Once she was out of his cologne-scented bathrobe and back into her familiar working clothes, she felt considerably better, more in control of herself and the situation. She looked into the mirror. The rain had caused her hair to fall into deep waves that clung close to her face and her eyes seemed larger than usual and more vulnerable. Worst of all, she saw the new Kareth lurking in their gray depths—the Kareth that had only come to the fore since she had met Lake Thorsen.

Resolutely, she set her chin at a stubborn angle. She had worked hard to fit the image of the efficient businesswoman. No woodcarver was going to re-arrange her life. With grim determination she picked up the bathrobe and walked briskly back to Lake.

"Here's your robe," she said in a businesslike tone. "It's getting late and I really ought to go now."

Lake gave her a long look, glanced at the mantel clock, then back to her. "Ten o'clock isn't terribly late."

"Nevertheless, I have a busy day tomorrow." She wished he wouldn't look at her with those soul-searching eyes. His perusal made her insides feel as wobbly as her knees.

Lake stood and took the robe she held out at arm's length to him. He held it up, looked at it inside and out, then shook it. "Okay, where is she? Where's the person who was sitting here a minute ago?"

Kareth clasped her hands in front of her like a child reciting a lesson. "I'm not that person. This is me—here."

"I don't believe you." He tossed the robe aside and took her in his arms. "No, I can see her. She's right there in your eyes, just waiting for a chance to come out."

"I—I have no idea what you're talking about. Let me go. I have to leave." Her heart was pounding and she had to struggle with herself to keep from throwing her arms about him and never letting him go.

Lake paid no attention to her empty words and listened to her soul. Tenderly, he lowered his head and took possession of her lips.

Kareth didn't struggle. There was no threat in his

embrace and even her discipline wasn't that perfectly controlled. Instead, she slipped her arms across the hard muscles of his back and opened her lips so their tongues could meet and caress.

When at last he released her, she gazed up at him in speechless wonder. Her world still whirled in pink gossamer clouds and she was perilously close to not leaving at all.

"Good night, Kareth," he said in a seductive tone that sent a tingle coursing through her. "Drive carefully and I'll see you tomorrow at three."

She nodded, not trusting herself to speak. Somehow she floated to the car and Lake closed her in securely. He tapped on the window and pointed at the door lock. When she pressed it down he stepped back and waved. As she drove away she looked back over her shoulder. Lake stood still in the misting rain, watching her go.

Kareth had never been one to lie, especially to herself, so by the time she reached her apartment she had examined her feelings thoroughly. Reasonable or not, expected or not, she was in love with Lake Thorsen. Now, what was she to do about it?

She parked her car and her city training had her out of the parking lot and halfway up her stairs, keys in hand, in a very short time. He might love her as well, she thought as she let herself in and automatically locked the door behind her. Certainly his eyes said he did, and his actions too. Words she disregarded. Anyone could say love words and she had heard enough lines to pay them little attention. But his eyes—his eyes spoke love.

Kareth switched off the lamp she had left burning and flicked on the hall light. At her bedroom she hesitated and looked about with new eyes. Had it always been so small? So lonely? She found herself wondering what Lake's bedroom was like. She assumed it was large since all the rooms she had seen were well-proportioned. Was his bed like the solid maple one she had used in his guest room? She didn't even know his favorite color.

Suddenly her phone rang, breaking off her thoughts. Sitting on her bed, she nudged off her damp shoes as she lifted the receiver. "Hello? Lake!" A sensation of warmth flowed over her.

"I just wanted to be sure you got home all right."

"Yes, I'm here." His mellow voice brought a sweet smile to her lips.

"Did you lock your door?"

"Of course. And there are no burglars under my bed."

"Then I'll see you tomorrow."

"Good-bye, Lake," she said happily.

"No. Never good-bye. Good night."

Kareth hesitated, to be sure her voice wouldn't tremble as it sometimes did when she felt a strong emotion. "Good night," she whispered, and gently hung up.

* * *

Kareth held the microphone toward the angular woman and tried to tilt her head in a way to keep her hair from obscuring her face. She had worn it down with a small barrette holding back the front, but a strong wind had blown up as soon as Charley started taping. The other woman, Alma Pritchett, was dressed in jeans and a cotton work shirt and was completely oblivious to the wind. A sudden gust swooped up Kareth's legs and she instinctively grabbed at her billowing skirt. Her action shifted the microphone, but she snapped it back up as Alma continued to speak. She hoped Lake hadn't noticed her problem. It was important to her, even more so now than usual, that everything go well with this interview. If Lake wasn't impressed with all this, he certainly wouldn't agree to let her tape him. Kareth glanced at Charley and was relieved that he had anticipated the problem and was shooting a close-up of the other woman.

"How old are these horses when you break them?" she asked as she fished a strand of hair out of her mouth.

"Break 'em? Hell, honey, there's nothing to break. As soon as they're born I start my handling. You know, pettin' 'em, leading 'em around. Every horse on this place is as tame as a pup." As if to prove her words, one of the huge Clydesdale mares dropped her head over the fence to nuzzle her mistress. "Just like Bessie here. A baby could crawl all over her."

"They sure are big," Kareth said with a hint of trepidation in her voice. "Those feet are the size of dinner plates."

Alma chuckled at Kareth's choice of words. "Those are called hooves, honey. No, the only animal on the place that I have to keep an eye on is my stallion there." She nodded toward a paddock behind them where an immense bay was penned. "They're sometimes traitorous."

"I see," said Kareth, who was again fighting to keep her heather-toned skirt down around her knees. As if that wasn't enough, a gust blew under the lapel of her mulberry-colored blazer, nearly stripping it off her shoulder and molding her cobalt-blue silk blouse to her breasts. Kareth turned her jacket back with a decorous movement.

"How long have you been raising these horses?"

As Alma Pritchett answered, Kareth risked a glance at Lake, who stood leaning against the white fence. He looked interested, but then the wind in her skirt might account for that.

"I've had horses most of my life. Bessie here is one of my oldest. She's twelve now. That one back there with the stallion is going on six years. She's in her prime."

Kareth glanced back at the penned mare, only to be blinded by hair whipping across her eyes. She turned back to Alma and went through the rest of her questions. She could tell by Charley's expression that he, too, was working hard to get just the right angle. She smiled confidently. Alma Pritchett was an interviewer's dream. If it weren't for the troublesome wind, she would be willing to stand here and talk all day. Kareth had always liked horses and the Clydesdales had a majesty about them that was similar to the grandeur of mountains.

Charley motioned to let Kareth know he was nearly out of videotape and she neatly summed up her show and thanked Alma for her time. Lake straightened, a broad grin on his face. After exchanging a few pleasantries with Alma, Charley lugged the heavy equipment to his car as Kareth walked with Lake to his dark blue sedan.

Once inside, Kareth sighed with relief. Her skin tingled from the whipping wind and her hair had fallen into tangles. By the time Lake slid behind the wheel she had extracted her brush from her purse and was attacking the rebellious masses.

"Well," she said with assurance in her voice, "how did you like it?"

"I thought it was very interesting. Especially your skirt."

She shot him a look of amused exasperation. "I meant the show."

"It was very informative. I know more about Clydesdales than I ever knew before, that's for sure."

"Alma Pritchett is wonderful. I think she could do her own series if we had enough tape. She never runs out of something to say." Kareth found her mirror and unsnapped her barrette and held it between her teeth. "Aren't those horses lovely? Every time I see them they take my breath away," she mumbled around the hair clip.

"They're spectacular all right." He seemed to be suppressing a grin. "Next time you do them, I'd like to watch again."

"Oh, we won't do them again." Kareth secured her hair with the clip.

"Yes, you will."

"No, there are enough interesting stories around here. We won't have to repeat them for a long, long time."

Lake was grinning openly now. "I'll bet you dinner at The Silver Bell that you'll tape them again in the very near future."

She looked at him. "I hate to take you up on that. The Silver Bell is pretty expensive." She wished she could take back her words. Lake might have no visible means of support, but he drove a nice car and his clothes were as elegant as those of anyone else she had ever dated. Today he wore chino slacks and a pullover of oyster and muted blues that could have been straight from Neiman's casual wear.

"That's okay with me if it is with you." He grinned smugly. "I won't have to pay off. But if you prefer somewhere else?"

"No, no. The Silver Bell is fine." She glanced across at him. "Do you have to go home now?"

"I thought we might take in a movie."

"With popcorn?" she bargained. "And butter?"

"Naturally. You can't see a movie without buttered popcorn."

"I think I could squeeze that into my busy schedule." She laughed.

"How about *The Creature That Walks?* I hear it's as scary as they come. Are you game?"

"You bet. If you can take it, so can I. I have to warn you, though, I'm a horror-film buff. I sat through *Mighty Joe Young* five times as a kid and have been hooked ever since."

"I grew up on *Frankenstein* and *Dracula*. I'll bet you're the first to flinch."

"You're on!" Kareth smiled broadly. She hadn't enjoyed anyone else's company so much in her entire life.

Kareth sat in the tape-editing room, a pad upon her crossed leg. On the white background of the editing viewer flickered numbers of black and gray. She scarcely noticed them. Lake was foremost in her mind. Lately he seemed to be lurking in her thoughts whether she was awake or asleep. Not that she minded. She was just going to have to get accustomed to walking around with a sappy grin on her face.

All at once she saw herself and Alma on the screen. Pulling her mind back to business, Kareth made a few notes, indicating which scenes should be shortened. One time she had asked a question that elicited a response almost identical to the previous answer. This was all standard. Charley had managed to avoid full-length shots that would show her rebellious skirt. Instead, he had focused in on torso and head shots.

Kareth smiled at Alma's homespun answers and easy camera presence. Then she glanced from her pad to the screen and back again. Her pen stopped moving and she stared back at the screen. The shot, her wrap-up of the interview, showed both her head and Alma's. Directly behind them in the center of the screen the huge Clydesdale stallion was claiming his conjugal rights with a mare as Kareth told the viewers she was certain this was one show she was sure they had enjoyed.

"Oh, damn," she moaned as her face flushed bright pink. "Double damn!"

She reached over and snapped off the equipment, not bothering to rewind the worthless videotape. Had it been any part but her wrap-up, she could have edited around it.

Tossing a pen and pad onto the table, she left the room. She had two calls to make. One, to reschedule an interview with Alma, the other, to make reservations for Lake and herself at The Silver Bell. Losing the bet was not easy for Kareth because of her inherently competitive spirit, but what she regretted even more was the fact that she had given Lake another excuse not to be on her show.

5

Lake relaxed back into The Silver Bell's wicker basket chair and regarded Kareth as she drank her coffee. She was the most beautiful woman he had ever known. Not just her face, though she was heartbreakingly pretty, nor her tall and lithe body, but her personality. She was beautiful inside, where it counted. He couldn't imagine Kareth saying or doing anything to hurt a person for her own selfish gain, even though she was very ambitious. He imagined that this was the real reason she was here in Livingston instead of living a star's life in Hollywood. Her looks would have been enough to get her the necessary attention, but, he surmised, the price of success out there must have been more than she was willing to pay.

She looked over at him through her long dark eyelashes. The candle's glow caught in her bright hair and made her creamy skin as translucent as fine porcelain. "What are you thinking?"

"I was just enjoying the sight of you. How you move when you drink your coffee, how you hold yourself when you don't know I'm watching. I'm memorizing you."

A faint blush warmed her cheeks and she lowered her eyes to study the hurricane-like swirl in her coffee cup.

"Did I embarrass you?" he asked. "I didn't mean to."

"No, not exactly. I'm just not accustomed to compliments."

"You're not? I would have thought you would hear them all the time." He leaned forward and covered her hand with his. He had once heard a very beautiful woman say she rarely dated and had married the first man who asked her because her appearance made men too shy to approach her. Was Kareth lonely too?

"I like this place," Kareth said to change the subject. "Whoever decorated it did a marvelous job."

Lake glanced around the large room. The theme was that of a mining camp in the gold rush days. Ore carts were used as table bases and the glass tops revealed chunks of "ore." An indoor fountain sent a constant stream of water down a wooden sluice to pool in a shallow quarry. Patrons had tossed in numerous pennies that gleamed brightly with the luster of gold, each representing a wish.

"The owner is a friend of mine," Lake told her. "He moved here from Colorado, as you might have guessed, and decided to bring a bit of it with him."

"I'm glad he did. The food is good, but the atmosphere alone makes it worth the trip out here. Why didn't he build his restaurant in town?"

Lake shrugged. "He owned this land and lives down the road about a mile. I guess he didn't want to have to drive too far to work." He smiled at her. "I could introduce you and you could do an interview with him."

"I would rather interview you." She gazed at him imploringly. "Won't you reconsider about being on my show? I have the perfect slot. I scheduled an interview with a man who had found a new use for old tires. At the time it sounded like a good idea, but when we taped him he came across as such an eccentric, I would rather not use the show. In retrospect, I guess he was more weird than interesting."

"Maybe I would be too."

She laughed. "You're not a kook—just terribly nice."

Lake studied her face in the candlelight. He didn't want to deny her anything. Besides, he told himself, she hosted a local show. For a few days people would recognize him and stop him to say hello when he came to town, but then it would all die down again. "All right," he said, "I'll do it."

"You will? You'll be on my show?" Kareth could hardly believe what she was hearing. Later she had planned to give him a big spiel about inspiring other young artists and here he was practically volunteering! A delighted smile lit her face. "That's wonderful!"

"But you have to promise you won't make me sound like some sort of nut. I've never been on television before."

"I would never do that to anybody, least of all you. Everything will work out fine. Can we do it tomorrow?"

"You sure don't let the grass grow, do you? Yes, let's do it tomorrow before I come to my senses again."

"I hope the weather is obliging. I'll check with Charley first thing in the morning and have him arrange for a camera tomorrow afternoon. Oh! I talked to the mayor today and he's thrilled over your loan of the Merlin for the park. He'll be contacting you in the next few days."

"Fine. Did he say where it will be exhibited?"

"We discussed it and he agreed with me that the end of the park with the grove of pin oak trees would be the best location. The man who designed the park will see to its placement if that's agreeable with you."

"As long as I don't have to do it."

"You won't have to worry about a thing. I'll plan it

so your TV interview airs about the same time as Merlin's debut."

"Whatever you say. Are you ready to go?"

She nodded and he stood to pull back her chair. At the cash register Kareth took out her credit card but Lake pushed it away. "This one's on me."

"But I lost the bet. I expect to pay."

"I tricked you, remember? I knew there was no way you could use that last part you taped."

"You're not playing fair."

"Next time I'll lose and you can pay." He pulled some bills from his pocket and paid their check without allowing her any further discussion.

"You cheat," she chided good-naturedly as they walked across the parking lot. "Cheaters never win."

"I wouldn't say that. I got to have supper with my favorite person in my favorite restaurant. I won, all right."

"I can't be your favorite person. Not yet. We hardly know each other."

"You expected several years chaperoned court-ship, followed by a slim volume of poetry, perhaps? These are the *nineteen* eighties, Kareth. Things move faster now."

"This fast? We're practically breaking the sound barrier."

"Do you want me to slow down? I could back off if you insist on it. We could see each other once, maybe twice a week, and then only for a movie or perhaps dinner and dancing. Someplace with lots of

other people. You'll have to insist upon it though."
They reached the car and he opened her door.

Kareth sat down and swung her long legs inside.
Lake waited outside, leaning his forearm on the car's
roof. "No," she said at last, "I don't want that."

They drove back toward town, each immersed in
their own thoughts. Above the rounded trees lightning flashed silently, making white and blue land-
scapes among the clouds.

"Heat lightning?" Kareth suggested.

"Seems a little early in the year for that. I think we
may be in for a storm."

Kareth looked out the window as another flash of
lightning arched from cloud to cloud. "It's easy to
see why people in ancient times thought the gods
were warring up there. Even now an electrical storm
is awesome."

Lake nodded and bent to glance out his window at
the rolling clouds. "Especially at night." He cast a
look in her direction. "Are you afraid of storms?"

"Me? No." She paused, then added, "Not much,
anyway."

They reached town and he drove her to her
apartment house. As they walked to the door thunder rumbled in the depths of the clouds, its voice that
of a caged beast breaking free.

Kareth shivered. A gust of air shook the bushes by
her door and made her wind chimes produce their
tinkling music. "Will you come in for a while? It's
early yet." She had lied. She was terrified of storms.

"Sure. I was hoping that would be all right with you."

She unlocked the door, and as they went inside, the lightning cast their shadows on the wall. "How about a glass of wine?" she offered.

"Great, if it's red and dry, or even if it's not," Lake replied as he looked around the room.

The apartment was small but tastefully decorated. To his left stood an apricot-colored sofa that looked invitingly soft and a recliner in a deeper shade of peach. A television set sat on an oak room divider along with numerous books and some bric-a-brac. A short hall led to what he assumed was the bedroom. On the right was a dining room furnished with only a rolltop desk and an upholstered straight chair. Beyond that was the kitchen, where he could hear Kareth getting down the glasses.

"I like your place," he called out to her.

"Thanks. Make yourself at home."

He went to the patio door that opened out on the apartment house quadrangle of grass and pool. Again lightning flashed, bathing the greenery in silver. He touched a collection of crystal prisms hanging beside the door, sending them dancing. He imagined that when the sun's angle was right the room would be full of rainbows from the crystals and would be splashed with even more color from a stained glass window that hung over the door's stationary side.

He turned back to ask Kareth if this was true, when suddenly the entire world was plunged into darkness. From the kitchen he heard the sound of a glass shattering on the floor, then a tightly spoken, "Oh, damn!"

"Stay still. I'm coming." As Lake felt his way through the blackness, he banged his knee on a chair and stumbled, but kept his balance and didn't fall. "Kareth? Where are you?"

"Here."

He reached out toward her voice and touched her hair. Pulling her closer, he said, "Are you hurt? You didn't cut yourself, did you?"

"No, no. I'm not hurt."

"You're trembling."

"Maybe." Her voice sounded wary, as if she half expected him to make fun of her.

"Honey, there's nothing to be afraid of."

"I know that." All at once an explosion of thunder surrounded them and Kareth threw herself into Lake's arms. "I hate storms," she confessed against his sport coat. "I always have."

"There now," he soothed her as if she were a frightened child. "I won't leave you."

Kareth clung to him while the storm raged overhead. One lightning bolt seemed to follow another as if electricity rained from the sky. Visions of every natural disaster possible scurried through her mind, sending all her rational thought stampeding away.

"Is it a tornado?" she managed to gasp, as this was the most likely catastrophe for the area.

"No, just a storm. Do you have candles?"

She nodded. "In my bedroom closet."

"You keep candles in the closet in your bedroom?" His tone was mirthful. "You're one kinky lady."

"No, I'm not. My kitchen is too small and I don't own a dining room suite. The candles are beside the tablecloths."

"Why do you own cloths and no table?"

"I have a card table—for guests," she explained.

"I knew there was a good reason. Lead me to your closet."

Keeping a firm grip on his hand, Kareth navigated her way down the hall. "Here," she said. "On the top shelf and toward the back."

Lake reached up and muttered as the same knee he had banged into the chair clipped a hard metal rim. "I found your card table. Are there matches?"

"There should be some by the candles."

He stretched up, feeling along the shelf. "You must not cook many meals for company. How do you reach this?"

"I stand on a chair."

His fingers closed over a thick waxy cylinder and he gave a cry of triumph. "I found one. And here's the box of matches."

Kareth heard a rattle and a scrape, and an acrid

smell filled the closet as Lake struck the match. She took the candle as he lit it and held it aloft so he could find others. One by one they lit the candles and soon the bedroom glowed with mellow, golden light.

"There!" Lake exclaimed as he set the last of the blazing candles on the dresser. "Do you feel better?"

"Yes. A little foolish, but better."

"Hey," he said gently as he came to her. "None of that. Everybody is afraid of something. That's just the way people are. Take me for instance—I'm scared to death of peanut butter milk shakes. I've tried to conquer it, but there it is."

A laugh bubbled up from Kareth in spite of her apprehension.

"See? I knew I could get you to relax." He smoothed her hair back from her temple.

"What are you really afraid of?"

Lake hesitated for a heartbeat. "I'm afraid you don't love me as much as I love you."

Kareth's lips parted incredulously and her eyes grew round.

"I hear you saying all this is happening too fast," Lake continued, "but I can't seem to stop it. I fell in love with you the first time I saw you. I know it's too soon and not reasonable, but I can't do a thing about it now. I love you."

"Lake," she said as she put her hand caressingly upon his chest. "I love you too."

Silence punctuated by the storm enveloped them. I shouldn't have admitted the truth so readily, she thought. Things *are* moving too fast.

"You do?" he finally asked. "You're sure you love me?"

"Yes." She nodded without hesitation. "I keep fighting it, but it won't go away."

"Oh, honey," he moaned with relief as he gathered her close. "Don't fight it. Let it happen."

"But I don't even know you. Not really," she protested as she held him tightly. "I don't even know your middle name or where you got that little scar on your thumb. Nothing!"

"I was never given a middle name, and the scar came from using a knife incorrectly. Now there's nothing to keep you from loving me."

She lifted her head and her tremulous smile met his. "I guess you're right. How about you? Any questions?"

"Just one. Do you have any regrets about splitting up with the man in California?"

"No. Not at all. I got over him months ago. I seldom think of him."

"That's all I wanted to know." He lowered his head and kissed her, almost shyly at first, then more surely.

Kareth felt her spirit soar to greet his and she was heady with the knowledge of his love. For once she gave her emotions a free rein and she was amazed at the surge of love she felt. When at last Lake's lips moved to her cheek and then to her hair, she whispered faintly over and over, "I love you. I love you." His arms were protectively strong about her, keeping her from swaying, and pressing her body close to his length.

"Kareth," he whispered as if her name meant love. "Kareth." He bent and lifted her with ease. Resting his knee on the bed, he laid her down. Her hair curled in a crown about her face and her slender arms reached up for him.

"Love me," she softly said.

"Are you sure?" he asked gently, not knowing what he would do about his surging need if she said no. "I don't want you to feel rushed."

"Rushed? I've wanted you since that first day I saw you."

He smiled as he lay beside her and pillowed her head on his arm. "Did you? When did you know you loved me?" he asked, voicing the age-old lover's question. "Was it right away?"

"No," she said teasingly. "I wanted you right away, but I didn't love you until much later. It happened about the time you first kissed me."

"You were just playing hard to get." He laughed with a deep resonance, then began nuzzling her neck. He raised his head and gazed into her eyes. "Kareth, do you really love me? That's not a word to bandy about lightly."

"I know," she replied genuinely. "I wouldn't say it unless I was sure I meant it."

He kissed her and tasted the sweetness of her breath warm in his mouth. Almost reverently he ran his hand over her side and cupped the full mound of her breast. His fingers caressed the soft globe as her nipple stiffened under his palm. Gently he squeezed the bud between his thumb and forefinger and Kareth moved against him encouragingly.

Slowly, deliberately, he drew his fingertips along the deep V of her neckline. Kareth threaded her fingers in his hair and guided his lips to follow his caress. Her skin was very warm and satiny on his lips. He breathed in deeply. The fragrance that was unique to Kareth filled his senses. He much preferred this to her perfume.

Pushing the silken fabric aside, he found her breast. He eased his finger just inside the lacy edge of her bra and she sighed eagerly in his ear. Her flesh was as velvety as a rose petal, and Lake had to restrain himself from proceeding too quickly.

"Kareth," he whispered as his lips moved over her warm cleavage. "How in the hell do you unfasten this dress?"

She laughed softly and took one end of the tie knotted at her waist. Slowly she pulled until the bow released. "It's a wraparound."

Lake brushed away the impeding fabric and lifted himself to one elbow. With ease he opened the front closure of her low-cut bra and swept away the wisp of fabric to reveal her perfectly formed breasts. For a long time he gazed at her as he traced his fingertips over her with the reverence he showed for a work of art. "You're even more beautiful than I expected," he said at last.

"Make love with me," Kareth implored, her smoky eyes meeting his. "Stay the night with me. Not because of the storm. But because I love you and I can't bear to be away from you."

Lake kissed her and her eager response had passion swirling through him. He tasted the delicateness of her inner lips and ran his tongue over the small ridges of her teeth. Wanting to know all her tastes and textures, he trailed butterfly kisses, accented by small licks, down her throat and lower to encompass her breast. When at last he claimed her nipple, Kareth moaned and arched toward him in passionate abandon.

Fires seemed to be coursing through her as his hot lips and even hotter tongue loved her breast and sent sharp urges throughout her entire body. His hand found her other breast and it, too, received his knowing attentions. His lips replaced his fingers and she drew her breath in quickly at the sensation. Her breasts had always been sensitive but her only other lover had scarcely touched them. Lake, however, kissed and licked and caressed her until she felt as if she were about to explode.

"You're wearing too many clothes," he said as he reluctantly lifted his head.

He eased away and pulled her to her feet. She stepped out of her shoes as he did the same and stood before him in the candlelight, her dress opened to the waist and her pouting breasts damp from his loving.

Lake smoothed the dress and bra from her shoulders. Caressingly he lifted her breasts as if their weight pleased him and rolled both her nipples between his thumbs and forefingers.

Kareth held her palms tightly against his waist, afraid to move for fear he would stop, yet so weak-kneed she was on the verge of falling.

"Lovely," he said softly.

He ran his hands down to slide her half slip down over her hips. Kareth, moving shakily in her passion, fumbled with the buttons of his shirt and finally succeeded in getting it off him. Taking as long as he had, she touched each sinewy muscle and hard ridge of his lean belly. His chest was bare and his own nipples were as coppery as pennies in the golden light. Kareth caressed the swelling of his biceps where veins flowed beneath the firm surface.

Lake ran his hands beneath the silken sheath of her panty hose and began to slide them down. Kareth swayed toward him and he kissed her deeply, longingly, as he lowered the garment. Kneeling, he stroked the nylon from her smooth legs and helped her step out of her hose, leaving only her lacy bikini panties to conceal the remainder of her body.

When he stood, Kareth unbuckled his belt and opened his slacks. As she lifted her face for his kiss she brushed his trousers down with her discarded clothing. In almost the same movement he removed his low-cut briefs and stood naked before her.

Almost shyly she let her eyes feast upon him and her lips tilted up in an appreciative smile. As her hands found him, he pulled her close and kissed her hungrily as if he would never get enough of her.

Lake turned her so that he sat on the bed and she stood between his legs. Alternately, he took first one of her breasts, then the other to his mouth and Kareth's head rolled back in ecstasy. With deliberate movements he pulled away her panties and cupped her firm buttocks in his hands, guiding her breasts to his seeking lips and tongue.

When Kareth was too weak to stand he lowered her to the bed and lay beside her, their bodies kissing from head to toe. She burned for him and wondered if the fire he had set blazing would ever be sated. Never before had she felt so eager to be loved nor so ready.

His large hands stroked over her hips and down her thighs and she willingly opened herself to him. His fingers found her and he murmured love words at the dewy sign of her readiness. In a continuous movement he rolled upon her and at last claimed her as his woman.

Kareth cried out in eagerness as he entered her and she held him closely as they moved together in the dance of love. Their bodies seemed to fit together perfectly and Kareth began to soar upward as Lake brought her greater and greater pleasure. Suddenly she seemed to take flight and she cried out again as she reached love's peak. Her release triggered his own and he held her tightly as wave after wave of completion pounded through them.

After what could have been moments but felt like a lifetime Kareth opened her eyes and dreamily met Lake's gaze. "I love you," she murmured.

"Marry me," he said.

"Marry? We don't know each other well enough."

His laugh burst out and she found herself laughing with him.

When she could speak she said, "When I marry, it will be forever, Lake. Let's be sure first."

"I'll be patient, but honey, this already is forever."

She smiled as he pulled her head to rest on his chest. In her heart she knew it too.

Kareth nudged Charley aside and looked through the lens of the softly humming camera. Lake stood by the water just as he had when she had first seen him. Beneath his skilled fingers the wooden unicorn became magic. Its heavy mane rose in a frozen breeze and its delicate head was turned slightly, as if it had just that moment heard a noise.

Kareth smiled and nodded to Charley. The angle, the light, everything was perfect. This would be her very best show. She was sure of it. Still smiling, she strode past the camera and toward Lake.

6

The show was a tremendous success!" Kareth announced as she ran from her car to meet Lake on his front porch. "The phones have been busy all day with people calling in about the program last night!"

"Good," Lake said with little enthusiasm. "Just the same, I wasn't all that pleased with the way I looked. I never noticed before how large my nose is."

"Nonsense. Your nose is perfect. No one likes the way they look on television. Your sculpture was magnificent. With the sun shining through the red buds that dragon looked as if it were alive."

"At least no one knows where I live. I'm beginning to understand why my parents became recluses." He met her on the top step and looped his arm companionably around her shoulder. "Did you miss me as much as I missed you all day?"

"Yes," Kareth admitted happily as she hooked her thumb in the belt loop of his jeans. "I get very little work done these days. All I can think about is coming out here to see you."

"I'm the same way. Marry me before we both go crazy."

She sat beside him on the porch swing and pushed it into motion with her toes. "I love you very much, Lake, and I want to accept your proposal, but I also need to wait awhile. All this has happened so quickly and is flaring so brightly, how do we know it won't burn itself out?"

"There are never any guarantees," Lake objected as he pulled her head down onto his shoulder. "We could wait ten years and still not be positive it would last."

"If we did marry, would you object to me continuing to work at the station?"

"Of course not. Why would I do that? I don't want to take away your identity or change you in any way—I just want to marry you."

Kareth looked up at him and kissed the lower part of his jaw. "You're too good to be true. I want to see if any chinks appear in your armor, Sir Knight."

From the den they heard the shrill ringing of the telephone. Lake sighed. "You aren't the only one who has had calls all day. Let's let it ring."

"You can't do that. What if it's something important?"

With an exaggerated sigh Lake got up. "Don't forget where we were—I was nagging you into marriage and you had your head on my shoulder."

"Got it," she said efficiently.

He crossed the porch with long, slow strides and after easing the screen door to so it wouldn't slam, he reached the phone on the fifth ring. Hoping the caller had hung up, he said, "Hello?"

"Hello, this is Chris Merriman. We've never met but I happened to see your sculpture on television last night." Her voice was businesslike and cultured, with sultry undertones.

"Thank you for telling me." He bent in preparation to hang up.

"I have recently bought several sites around the country with the intention of constructing a series of amusement parks. For months I've tried to decide on a central theme and until I saw your interview I had no really inspiring ideas. Mr. Thorsen, I would like to discuss commissioning you to supply the sculptures for my chain of parks which I will call the Enchanted Woods."

"Amusement parks?" Lake repeated. "You want me to carve pieces for them?"

Kareth had followed him inside and she nodded eagerly, pantomiming that he should agree.

"I don't know, Ms. Merriman. That sounds like a

big project and I don't have very many sculptures on hand."

"I'll tell you what," the voice suggested, "I have to fly back to my home in St. Louis in a few hours, but I could come back to meet with you, say, in the latter part of next week? We can discuss price and schedules and I can see your work for myself. What day would you prefer?"

Lake looked at Kareth, who was gesturing excitedly. "How about next Thursday?" He gave her directions to his house and said good-bye.

"Someone wants to buy some carvings?" Kareth prompted as he hung up.

"More than that. She said she wants me to do the theme animals for a series of amusement parks."

"Really! How wonderful!"

"I don't know about that. I've never sold my work nor had to produce to meet a schedule. All this is really very flattering, but I'm not so sure I want to, or even can."

"If she wants your carvings, I'm sure all that can be worked out."

Lake looked at her with no conviction at all. "I wouldn't even know what price to ask."

Kareth thought for a minute. "I interviewed an artist a few months ago. If you'd like me to, I'll call and ask him how he sets his prices."

"That might be a good idea. She'll be here next Thursday. She said to look for her at four o'clock. Kareth, I don't want to do this."

"Oh, but Lake! Think what it could mean to your career!"

He frowned and turned to the window.

Kareth went to him and put her arm around his waist. "Look at it this way. You're going to be carving anyway. It might as well bring in money."

"Damn it, I told you I don't need the money," he said sharply.

"Unless you're secretly the president of a million-dollar corporation or something, you can use the money!" she snapped back.

Unexpectedly Lake laughed. "No, I'm not president of anything, but . . ."

"Then that's that. If I did agree to marry you, I assume there would be little Lakes and Kareths that would need to be fed, clothed, and educated. Put the money aside for that."

Having fully recovered from his flare-up, Lake asked, "Do you really want me to do this? Seriously?"

"Certainly! What do you think I'm saying to you?"

"All right. I'll talk to her. But don't assume I'm going to agree to do the carvings. Okay?" His eyes were alight with devilment as he continued. "In the meantime, you can help me with another of my curiosities."

"What's that?" Kareth asked.

"Just tell me one thing. If a little lake is a puddle, what's a little Kareth?"

She grinned. "Enough to keep you in line and doing what's best for your career."

"Thank you, Mother," he said dutifully. "Go take a flying leap off the porch."

"Hey, don't get mad at me. I'm only trying to help you."

"I know. I know. It's just that I don't necessarily want to be helped."

He guided her back out and sat her in the swing. Putting her head on his shoulder, he said, "I believe this is where we were when we were interrupted. I was convincing you to marry me."

"And I was saying that I might, but I want to get to know more about you first. I don't even know how you earned your living in Houston."

"Well, that's easy enough to clear up. I—" Again the jangle of the phone sounded. "I'm going to let the damned thing ring."

Kareth looked in the window beside the swing. "Don't you want to know who it is?"

"No."

Once more the ring rent the air.

"I can't stand the sound of an unanswered phone. It might be a long-lost aunt or uncle trying to contact you."

"None of my relatives is lost and every one of them knows I detest talking on the phone."

"Maybe it's someone looking for me. I gave your number to the station in case of an emergency."

"All right," he gave in reluctantly. He answered

the phone and Kareth heard him say, "No, I'm not interested in starting a class in sculpting. No, ma'am, I don't know a thing in this world about pottery. Yes, ma'am. Good-bye."

Before he could leave the room the phone rang again.

"Hello? A bus tour of the grounds? You have the wrong number." He hung up abruptly, only to have the phone resume ringing. "Hello!" he snapped. Then, "Kareth, it's for you."

She went inside and took the receiver. "Hello?"

"Miss Langley? This is William McBlair with the American Broadcast System. I saw your program last night about the sculptor and I wondered if you would be interested in having the network pick it up for a single showing."

Kareth clapped her hand over the mouthpiece. "It's somebody from ABS!" she hissed at Lake. Assuming more aplomb, she said to Mr. McBlair, "Yes, Mr. McBlair. I would indeed be interested."

"I'll be in Houston tomorrow. Could you come down and meet with me? Say about nine tomorrow morning?"

"Tomorrow?" she said doubtfully. That was Friday and she had planned to take the day off and spend it with Lake.

"I'm afraid that's the only time I'll be available. I have other meetings scheduled from noon on and I fly out again at seven."

Lake covered the receiver and whispered, "You

aren't working tomorrow! I'm taking you away from these phones."

"Where?" she asked Lake.

"To Galveston. We're going to walk barefoot on the beach and forget there are any such things as television stations and telephones."

"Can we go down tonight?"

"Hang up and we're on our way. I'll go pack."

Kareth smiled as Lake strode away. This was a big opportunity, a network showing. "Mr. McBlair? Yes, nine o'clock will be fine. Where should I meet you?"

Kareth glanced at her wristwatch for the dozenth time and leaned toward the driver of the Space City cab. "Could we go a little faster?"

"Sure, lady. You get out and tell all these cars to get out of our way and I'll prepare for takeoff."

Kareth sighed and leaned back against the plastic seat cover. Cars were creeping by in a traffic snarl and it was already nearly eleven-thirty. She had hoped to be back from her appointment with William McBlair before Lake woke up and saw she was gone.

At least, she tried to console herself, the meeting with Mr. McBlair had gone well and she had found him to be a personable and direct man with a keen business sense. He had also been long-winded, however, and she had been agonizingly aware of the minutes ticking away. Still, one didn't rush a producer at ABS. Not when one wanted national coverage. This would be a fantastic opportunity, not only for

Lake, but for her station and for herself. She gloated silently over the coup she had garnered. Lake would be thrilled when she told him.

The cars edged past an eighteen-wheeler that had jackknifed in the middle lane. Kareth noticed that the traffic in the opposite direction, though not impeded by the overturned truck, was moving almost as slowly as her lane because of the drivers who craned their necks to see the wreck. Kareth shook her head in amazement. People fascinated her. She had often said she could watch them for hours, but until now she'd never really had the time to do so.

Once they were past the traffic bottleneck their speed picked up. The cab driver seemed determined to make up for lost time and Kareth wondered if she dared ask him to slow down a little.

When they reached the motel she slid out and paid him, then hurried across the thickly carpeted lobby and down the hall. There wasn't the slightest chance that Lake could still be asleep, but Kareth hoped he had found her note and wasn't worried.

As soon as she fit the key into the lock the door opened and Lake glared down at her. "Where in the hell have you been?" he demanded.

"Didn't you read my note?"

"Yes, it says, 'I'll be back soon.' Was that supposed to keep me from worrying?"

"As a matter of fact, it was." She sat on the rumpled bed and smiled up at him beguilingly. "Guess where I've been."

"I've tried to guess that for hours!"

"I've been with William McBlair," she stated triumphantly.

"Is that supposed to be good news? Who is he?"

"Why, he's the man from ABS. You heard me get the call yesterday."

Lake gave her a sideways look. "And?"

She beamed up at him. "You're going to be on nationwide television!"

"What!"

"I knew you'd be excited. The network has picked up the show and it will air next month."

"No way. I'm not going to do another show for anybody!"

"You don't have to. They'll use the one we already taped." She bounced on the side of the bed in her enthusiasm. "Isn't that great? It will mean bonuses for Charley and myself—maybe even a raise. Unlike you, I enjoy making money."

Grudgingly Lake said, "I'm glad for you and for Charley."

"You should be happy for yourself as well," she chided him. "Most artists would kill for a chance to be on national television."

"Let me try to explain." He sat beside her on the bed. "I'm a very private person. I don't want national recognition. I've had my fill of big cities and the rat race. I just want to live in my house in the Big Thicket and not be bothered by anyone who isn't a friend."

"Do you want to be bothered by friends?" she teased.

"You know what I mean. I appreciate what you're trying to do, but I don't want it. Find someone else to discover. I'm even willing to help you look, but don't pick me."

"Too late," she said, nudging his neck with her nose. "I already did it and you're a big success."

He sighed and pulled her back on the bed. "You're as hard-headed a woman as I've ever met."

"And fun?" she fished gleefully.

"Yes."

"And sexy?"

"Completely."

"And intelligent? Wise? Witty?"

"What are you doing—hunting for compliments?"

"Who, me?"

"Well, you aren't getting any more from me. At least not right now. You've turned my life into a three-ring circus and I'm trying to be mad at you."

"Oh?" she said innocently as she ran her tongue over his ear. "Are you succeeding?"

"Not entirely."

"Then let's go to the beach." Without waiting for him to agree, she jumped up and started changing from her tailored suit to a pair of shorts.

Lake leaned back and watched her appreciatively. "I may give you a few more compliments."

Kareth shrugged out of her blouse and half slip and smiled. "Such as what?"

Lake reached out and caught her wrist. "I can't tell you way over there. Come here." He pulled her to the bed and capsized her onto him. "There. That's much better."

She propped her forearms on his chest and peered down her nose at him. "First tell me you aren't mad at me anymore."

"I haven't quite decided."

"Tell me or else."

He grinned. "First you desert me, then you make my life open to the nation, now you threaten me."

"Okay, you asked for it!" In a lithe movement Kareth sat astride him and tickled his ribs.

Lake gave a whoop and tried to grab her fast-moving hands without hurting her or letting her continue to taunt him. When he anchored her hands he rolled over on her and pinned her arms above her head.

"Give up?" she asked.

Chuckling, he bent and kissed her long and hard. "You sexy broad," he growled as he nibbled his way over her breast. Holding her hands in one of his, he freed the front fastener of her bra and took one of her nipples into his mouth.

Kareth moaned with pleasure and closed her eyes to savor the urgent passions he awoke. When she could speak she said, "After last night I thought I would be satisfied forever and here I am wanting you again."

"Insatiable hussy," he mumbled against her breast. "I guess we'll just have to do it all over again."

"If we must, we must," she agreed with pretended reluctance. "Oh, yes, do that!" She arched against him as he sent love's fire surging through her.

Suddenly there was a loud knock on the door and both Lake's and Kareth's heads swiveled toward it.

"Are you expecting someone?" he asked.

"No, are you? I was gone a long time."

"Not long enough for me to meet someone, fall in love, and ask her to drop by."

The knock sounded again. "Maybe it's the vice squad," he hissed in a melodramatic whisper. "How old are you?"

"Too old for any vice squad I ever heard of. Maybe you ought to ask who's there?"

He was saved the trouble by a loud female voice. "Hello. You in there? This is housekeeping." The voice was both impatient and heavily accented.

"Can you come back later?" Lake asked as his hand stroked Kareth's bare breast.

"I no can do that. I get off work. You stay next day, you tell front desk or you pay anyway. Checkout one o'clock."

"All right," Lake groaned. "We'll get out by one."

Kareth looked at her watch. "It's five till now."

He collapsed onto her, muttering an expletive under his breath. "What perfect timing. Think you can hold this mood until we get to Galveston?"

"Probably. I've been in this mood ever since we met."

They dressed hastily and tossed their belongings into their bags. After a quick check to be sure they were leaving nothing behind, Lake opened the safety lock. The disgruntled maid glared at them as they edged past her.

"Have a good day," Lake called over his shoulder.

She muttered something in a foreign language as she drew her cleaning cart to block the door.

"A lovely person," Lake commented blithely as they got into his car. "A beam of sunshine in this dreary world."

They drove south and the bustle of Houston gradually dwindled to a more sedate pace. The flat land stretched out along both sides of the freeway and the only undulations in the road were the overpasses.

"It's a big change from Livingston, isn't it?" Lake commented. "Not a hill in sight."

"I grew up in Amarillo. I'm used to flat land."

"You did? Thought you were from California."

"No, I moved there after college."

"See? I didn't know that about you, but I was willing to marry you. I told you we can work out these little details. They could even add spice to our lives. I won't tell you the name of my first grade teacher until, say, our fifth anniversary. You don't have to tell me about your first date until our golden anniversary."

"You goose." She laughed. "If you keep plying me with all these flowery words, you'll turn my head."

"I'm going to do better than that. I'm fixing to sweep you off on an ocean cruise."

"The boat had better float fast. I have to be at work Monday."

"It's a small ocean. We're going to ride on the ferry across to Bolivar Peninsula and feed the sea gulls."

Kareth sighed happily and rested her hand on his thigh. "I love your method of sweeping me off my feet. Maybe I'll marry you after all. Someday."

7

Lake watched Kareth nervously pace the floor, pause yet again to look out the window, then continue her pacing. "I wish you would sit down and relax," he told her with some irritation. "It's not the President of the United States—just someone who wants to buy wood carvings."

"Oh, no," she protested. "It's much more important than that! Don't you see? This could be the beginning of a fantastic career!"

"Honey"—he motioned for her to sit beside him on the couch—"I keep telling you I don't want a career."

Kareth frowned but she perched on the edge of the cushion. "I think that's a very irresponsible attitude. If I thought the way you do, I'd still be in Amarillo working in my father's store. A person has to grab opportunities as they appear. Who knows when it will be too late? Opportunities only knock once. This could be your very best chance for a wonderful, stupendous career!"

"Do you realize that if I took away your superlatives and platitudes, we wouldn't be having a conversation?"

"There's no need to insult me," Kareth replied huffily. "Platitudes became platitudes because they're true."

"Not always."

"I forget, Mr. Thorsen, that you live in a different world. Tell me, sir, how do you plan to exist without money? No, don't tell me—squirrels will bring you nuts and berries to tide you over your hard times."

"Now who's being insulting?" he demanded. "I'm not saying a person should lie around and do nothing. That's not what I believe at all. I'm only trying to tell you I don't care whether or not this Chris Merriman buys my work."

Kareth felt her temper rise and she was forming a scathing retort when she heard a car stop out front. "She's here!"

Lake uncoiled his length from the couch and started toward the door.

"No, no! Wait until she rings the bell," Kareth said, catching his arm.

"That's silly."

"No, it's not. You don't want her to think you're too eager."

"I don't really think there's much chance of that." The sound of the doorbell pealed throughout the house. "Should I answer it now or do we wait until she's started back to her car? Better yet, we wait until she drives away, run across the field, and flag her down on the road."

"Just open the door," Kareth snapped.

She watched Lake cross the small entryway and open the front door. He was so dear to her, yet when it came to business he simply didn't play with a full deck. Kareth smiled and shook her head lovingly. Luckily he had her to help him.

Chris Merriman came into the hallway and Lake motioned toward Kareth. "This is Kareth Langley, Miss Merriman. She is sort of my business manager."

Kareth sent him a reproving glance and held out her hand in greeting. The young woman was tall and slender with auburn hair and pale green eyes. Her adobe tan suit fit perfectly and her ivory blouse was neither too tailored nor too frilly. The oxblood leather attaché case she carried perfectly completed the image of an efficient and self-assured business woman. Kareth said, "It's so good of you to come all the way out here. Did you have trouble finding your way, Miss Merriman? It is *Miss* Merriman, isn't it?" When she had pushed Lake into this meeting, she'd had no idea the woman would be so beautiful.

"It is miss, but call me Chris," she insisted. "No, I had no trouble at all getting here." She looked around at the log walls and tasteful color scheme. "I admire your house, Mr. Thorsen. I don't believe I've ever been inside a modern log cabin before."

"Let's not be so formal," Lake said with a grin. "You can call us by our first names, too, Chris. I'm glad you like my house."

"Let's show her the carvings," Kareth interjected. She didn't like the way Chris was smiling up at Lake with her perfect teeth and penetrating eyes. Not even a single strand of her stylish hair was out of place.

They left the house and went down the trail toward the wooden bridge. Kareth found herself lagging behind, watching Chris converse with Lake about his log house and the extent of his lands, as well as his training in the field of sculpture. Jealousy pricked Kareth. It really wasn't any of Chris's business whether Lake was native to the region or whether he liked to travel.

They crossed the rough-hewn bridge and, as Kareth had weeks before, Chris drew in her breath with surprise when she confronted the troll. From that angle the dragon was almost hidden by brush and as they left the bridge, the huge beast came into view.

"Magnificent!" Chris exclaimed. "They're even better than I had hoped."

"The dragon isn't for sale," Lake explained, "and even if it was, I'm not sure it could be removed since it's curled around several trees."

"I had thought perhaps the carvings for the Enchanted Woods should be done of native wood," Chris said as she ran her manicured fingers over the rough scales.

"That would be best. Then the animals will blend in with their surroundings," Lake agreed. "I'm assuming, of course, your locations have trees."

"Yes, so far they are all untouched. I would like you to give me some input as to how we should lay out the parks. A merry-go-round can be set up on any level surface. However, I want banks of trees and shrubbery to hide one area from another."

"I like the idea." Lake nodded. "Amusement parks erected on acres of concrete don't appeal to me, and my carvings wouldn't look right there. The setting is important when you're talking about dragons and unicorns."

"Lake has a Merlin at the city park," Kareth put in eagerly.

"I could sell you that one. Of course it will be a month before it will be released. If you'd like, I can draw you a sketch of it."

"It stands seven feet tall," Kareth added.

"I'd love to see it," Chris acknowledged, turning to look directly at Lake. Kareth didn't miss the gesture.

They went to the small meadow where Kareth had

first seen Lake. The unicorn seemed to have lifted its head at their approach, and the three fairies leaped in frozen glee over the large mushroom.

"You have an enchanted woods of your own," Chris exclaimed. "I see what you mean about the setting being important. Good heavens! The deer are carved! I thought for a minute they were real."

"I made a similar mistake when I saw Lake," Kareth put in. "I thought he was a statue. I was wrong," she finished lamely. She was feeling more and more like an unnecessary third party, especially when Chris smiled coolly and cast an appraising glance at Lake.

"I can see how wrong you were," Chris said smoothly.

"I could carve fairies and mushrooms easily," he explained, his attention on his work. "Also some large flowers—like two-foot tulip blooms or roses—that sort of thing. That doesn't take much wood and I can get several from one tree. The deer or dragon are a little different. I prefer to work with just one very large tree, otherwise the wood from several must be bonded together. And since all the wood in a statue must look like it's from the same source, I have to find trees with wood grains that very closely match, and sometimes that isn't easy."

"The only place we may have trouble with the wood is my West Texas location," Chris said thoughtfully. "It has only mesquite trees."

"If I can get cedar from somewhere else, it will be

close enough to fit in," Lake suggested. "I can use the native wood wherever possible and fill in with similar materials when necessary. Also, the carving must be scaled to the setting." He gestured at the huge trees. "I can put anything in a forest this size, but we may want to stick to unicorns and fairies for the mesquite. Nothing should stick up over the top of the trees." He caught his lower lip in his teeth and stood thoughtfully with his thumbs hooked in his jeans. "I might do a sleeping dragon, though."

"Perfect! I *knew* you were the one for the job. Your ideas and mine are so closely attuned."

"If you have a location near here, I would like to interview you for the grand opening," Kareth offered. "It's only a local show, but it would be good publicity."

"That would be nice. I have a location I'm considering here in East Texas near Henderson. I haven't purchased the property yet, so I'd appreciate it if you didn't tell anyone before I have time to complete the transaction."

Kareth looked a little crestfallen. "Henderson is out of our viewing area. Still, I'll talk to the station owner. He may feel it's time-worthy anyway."

"I would appreciate that. Tell me, Lake, how long would it take you to do, say, six carvings?"

"It depends on the size. A dragon may take several months. These fairies, maybe a few weeks. Also weather is a factor. Because of their size I usually work outside."

"Some of them, like the giant Viking, are still embedded in the ground, roots and all," Kareth said.

"I see."

Chris's cool politeness made Kareth feel as if she were somewhat in the way, like a precocious child. Kareth managed to keep her features unruffled but she knew it was only due to her acting ability. "What price did you have in mind?" she asked. At once she realized her words fell awkwardly into the conversation. "I mean, so far you haven't mentioned that at all."

Chris's finely arched brows lifted. "Ah, yes, I recall Lake said you are his business manager." Her smile never quite reached her light eyes. Calmly she named a six-figure sum.

Kareth swallowed. "That's less than we had expected. I had twice that much in mind."

"All right," Chris answered. "I'll double my offer."

Kareth nearly stumbled but said to Lake, "Is that figure agreeable to you?"

Lake stared at them both as if he could scarcely believe what he was hearing. "Sure. That's more than fair."

"Now, remember," Chris added, "I'll also pick up your travel expenses as well as food and lodging."

"What travel?" Kareth asked. "What lodging?"

"Perhaps you didn't hear me when I said I wanted the carvings made from woods that grew in the area of each park."

"Can't you ship the wood here?" Kareth faltered.

"Ship an entire tree? Not on my budget. Paying for Lake's food and lodging would be less expensive. Not to mention the fact that he will be able to produce exactly the right creature if he's carving it on location."

"How long did you say a dragon takes?" Kareth asked Lake.

"Two or three months by the time I factor in rainy days." He smiled at her maddeningly. "But it's just part of furthering my career," he teased.

Kareth frowned. "I hadn't thought of this in terms of travel."

"Why, I thought you had it all planned out," he responded innocently. To Chris, he said, "Let's shake hands on these preliminary terms and you send me a contract as soon as you can. Okay?"

"You have yourself a deal," Chris agreed, holding out her slim hand.

Kareth's frown increased and she found she had a tight knot in the middle of her stomach. "Will you be on location as well?" she asked Chris.

"Oh, yes. While Lake is doing the carvings I'll be overseeing the actual building of the park. My home is in Missouri but lately I haven't seen much of it, and likely won't until the first park is finished." She smiled at Lake and now her eyes lit with happiness. "I'll look forward to working with you. Expect a contract from my lawyer in a week or so."

"I'll be looking for it," Lake replied as he released her hand.

Kareth followed them silently up the trail. Her thoughts were dark as she heard them plan to begin the parks in Colorado Springs. She managed to bid Chris a civil good-bye, but as the woman drove away Kareth anxiously turned to Lake.

"Do you realize that if it takes you three months to carve a dragon and maybe two to make a unicorn, it will take you *years* to complete that contract?"

He nodded. "You won't have to worry about me for a long time. I appreciate your help in the price negotiations. I probably would have settled for the first sum Chris offered."

His easy use of the woman's name stung Kareth. "*Years*, Lake. That's a long time between dates!"

"This was your idea, honey. I tried to talk you out of it. Besides, I'll fly in from time to time." He walked over to the big oak and sat down in the masses of bluebonnets. "Have you ever looked closely at these? They really do look like tiny old-fashioned bonnets."

"Don't change the subject." She sat down beside him. "Do you want to see me so seldom?"

"No. I want you to marry me and accept me just as I am. Right now—not in several months or years or however long it takes you to decide our love is permanent. That's what I want."

Kareth felt her breath stick in her throat. "All the time you're away from me, you'll be with her."

"Chris? She did say she would be there. After all,

she has to see that everything goes just the way she wants it."

"She's sort of pretty, isn't she?"

"I guess you could say that."

"I wonder how old she is."

Lake shrugged and twirled a tiny stalk of flowers between his thumb and forefinger. "About my age, I would imagine." He paused. "Her eyes were an unusual color, weren't they?"

"Too pale. And I'll bet she dyes her hair."

"Who cares as long as it's attractive?" Lake commented. "Do you dye yours?"

Kareth blushed and touched her hair self-consciously. "Once in a while I use a rinse to give it body. Just a rinse—not dye."

"It looks good," Lake said with a grin. "And natural."

"It *is* natural! I don't alter the color." She threw a flower at him. "Don't change the subject. We were talking about your career."

He put his arms around her neck and touched his forehead against hers. "I would much rather talk about you. The subject is more interesting."

Kareth's unhappy gray eyes met his and the corner of her mouth twitched despondently. "I wish you hadn't shaken hands with her. Do you suppose that's binding?"

"I've promised to do the carvings. I'm sure there will be something in the contract to negotiate though. There always is."

"Then you'll be away for years." Her voice was as miserable as her expression.

"You sound as if I'm gone already. Give me a smile."

"I can't. I don't think I have any left."

He put his curved forefinger under her chin and tilted her head up. "I'll bet you have a smile left in there somewhere." Gently he kissed her, then drew back to look at her. "Let's try again." Once more his lips closed over hers and he ran the tip of his tongue over her lips until they parted.

Wrapping his arms around her, Lake placed her in the cushiony bluebonnets and stretched out beside her. "I love you," he murmured in her ear.

Don't leave me, she whispered back in her mind. Yet she couldn't say the words aloud. She had had her chance for fame and now it was Lake's turn. If she kept him from this, she might never forgive herself, and in the years to come it could become a source of trouble if he felt the same way. "I'm so happy for you," she said instead as she held him tightly and closed her eyes to restrain her tears.

Lake drew back a little and looked at her. "You are?"

"Yes, it's a marvelous opportunity. The sort of thing that may not come along again." She pulled him back into her embrace as she felt a tear gather and slide down her cheek.

"I'm glad you're happy," Lake said in a confused

voice. "For a minute there I thought you wanted me to back out."

"And lose the chance of a lifetime? No." She molded her body to his, heedless of the fact they lay in his front yard. Under the guise of pushing her hair out of her eyes, Kareth brushed away the tear. "I love you with all my heart and I want you to have the best of everything."

Lake again found her lips and Kareth kissed him hungrily, as if she could store up memories to tide her over his long absences. "Don't you dare look at that Chris Merriman," she warned.

"Why would I want her when I have you? Anyway, she seems to be a logical sort of person and I'm getting accustomed to you."

Kareth had to smile then and Lake rolled over and over, holding her close until she burst into laughter.

"Make love with me," he challenged her.

"Here? In the front yard?"

"You sound as if we're in downtown Los Angeles. Why not? I'm not expecting company and we're out of sight of the road."

"Here?" she repeated. But she smiled at the idea. "I've never made love outside before."

"Neither have I. We'll be having a first time experience together." He sat up and started unbuttoning her blouse.

After a brief hesitation Kareth began opening his shirt and the race was on to see who could undress the other the quickest.

"I won!" Lake announced triumphantly.

"No, I did!" She whacked him across the shoulder with his sock.

"We'll call it a tie," he compromised, "even if I did finish first."

Kareth lay back on the bluebonnets and spread her arms. "Whoever would have guessed a bed of flowers would be so prickly?"

"Here. Lie on my clothes." Lake spread his shirt and jeans to make a pallet. "Is that better?"

Kareth answered by smiling and pulling him down to her. "I hope you have plenty of time because I plan to ravish you."

"Do as you must and don't worry about being gentle," he said, submitting gracefully. "Only respect me in the morning."

He was as handsome as a Greek god as he leaned toward her, his golden hair lifting in the breeze and his eyes rivaling the leaves of the flowers. A series of white clouds lined the sky and silhouetted Lake.

"I'm lucky to be loved by you," Kareth whispered. All her thoughts of his upcoming travel had been set aside and her full attention was fixed on the only man who had ever really loved her.

Lake gazed down at her. Her dark red-gold hair was spread into a crown of flames burnished by the sun. Amid the bluebonnets her skin was pale and glowing, as if she were a jewel surrounded by amethysts and emeralds. Her eyes were the deep gray that he knew signaled her most keenly felt emotions. He wondered if she was telling the truth when she said she wanted him to go through with the deal with Chris Merriman. She certainly seemed convinced.

Lake kissed her slowly, savoring all the love she gave him and enjoying the twin peaks of her breasts as they teased his chest. He ran his hand up her thigh, over the curve of her hip and the valley of her waist, to cup one luscious globe in his palm. Kareth moved eagerly beneath him and he glided his hard palm over her nipple. He had quickly learned that her breasts were unusually sensitive and that she enjoyed having him touch them. He was more than happy to oblige.

Trailing kisses down her neck, he tasted the faint saltiness of her skin. A pulse beat rapidly in her throat and he licked it lovingly in passing. His kisses brushed the firm skin of her upper chest as he made his way to the softness of the rounded flesh of her breasts. Lake nuzzled in the sun-warmed cleavage and nibbled his way over to one coral-tinted center.

He drew back and for a few seconds he watched the taut prize as his fingers toyed with it. The sun left a sheen on the tempting curve of her pale flesh. Topping it was the bud that seemed to draw him magnetically. Slowly, as though he might yet change his mind, Lake returned to lick her nipple. Kareth's body arched toward him and he rewarded her by taking it into his mouth and drawing at it gently. Her skin felt smooth and surprisingly cool except for the hard nub against his tongue.

Lake stroked her flat stomach, dipped his finger into the shallow depression of her navel, and ventured downward to the thick mass of curls. Kareth eagerly opened herself to him and he found her invitingly ready. With the expertise of a perfect lover his fingers began to arouse her to greater and greater passion. When he felt she could bear waiting no longer, he altered his position and entered her. Continuing the same rhythm, he heard her cry out and felt the steady contractions of her fulfillment.

With barely controllable desire Lake kissed her thoroughly, drawing her full lower lip into his mouth and running his tongue into the warm recesses. When he again felt Kareth begin to quicken to his loving, he rolled over, pulling her on top of him.

She sat back, holding her weight upon her knees and bracing her palms upon his chest. The sunlight tangled in her bright hair and glowed over her full breasts. Lake put his hands on her hips and guided her in their motions of love. When she took up the movement he slid his hands higher to cup both her breasts.

Almost at once Kareth's head rolled back and her eyes closed. Her lips parted as if they had been kissed and he heard the soft moan that signaled her imminent release. Letting all his barriers slip, Lake joined her in her completion and together they soared and spiraled in the climax of their loving.

Kareth put her arms around Lake and let him roll her so that they lay on their sides, neither willing to break their bond, neither aware of the scent of the wild flowers or the prickling of their skin from the bluebonnets. A sweet smile tilted both their lips, and their souls still seemed to be merged into one.

"I will always," Kareth murmured, "love bluebonnets."

"So will I. We can both be glad the state flower isn't a rose. Those thorns would be hell at a time like this."

Kareth laughed into the curve of his neck. "Cactus flowers would be even worse." She met his eyes and grew solemn as the thoughts she'd tried to ignore crept back into her consciousness. "I'm going to miss you."

"Hush," he admonished her gently. "Let's not talk about that now. All I want to hear you say is how much you love me."

"I don't think I realized how much until today. I truly love you more than I love myself." Otherwise, she finished silently, I could never let you go.

"You're everything to me," he told her softly as he stroked her hair back from her face. "I never knew I could love so much."

Kareth turned her head on the pillow of his arm and kissed his sun-warmed shoulder. She knew it would take all her will power to refrain from asking him to call off the deal with Chris Merriman, yet she couldn't be a millstone around his neck. "I'm going to be so proud to know your sculptures are all over the country. Maybe on my vacation you can take me around and show me all the sites."

Lake sighed and gave her an undecipherable look. "We had better get dressed before you have a very uncomfortable sunburn."

She reached for her clothes and wondered if he was so excited about his new career that he didn't want to waste any time before starting the preliminary sketches. She had never been fond of amusement parks and now she suspected she would learn to hate them.

8

The walls of the odd house glowed with their own light and Kareth looked around her in amazement. "I can certainly say I've never seen a house quite like this, Mr. Cheevey. Where did you get all these bottles?" She directed the microphone at her guest.

The khaki-clad man peered about his glass house. "I found them here and there. By the roadside mostly. Before I retired I was a county bridge inspector. Used to go all over checking bridges. Under every bridge I'd find a mess of bottles. At first I brought the bottles home and tossed them out back." He fixed her with an accusatory eye. "They make an awful mess by the roadside, you know."

"Yes, I can see how they would." Kareth ran her fingers over the slick bottle necks. They all faced inside, with the exception of a few by the front door that were used to hang A. D. Cheevey's carved wooden name plaque outside.

"I put corks in these," he went on to explain. "I use them like a bulletin board, or to hang pictures on. Eventually I guess I'll find corks for all of them. That will insulate it better, don't you know?" He looked with pride at his living room/bedroom combination. "Don't need no windows. All you have to do is look through a clear jar." He peered through a mason jar, surrounded by amber beer bottles. "I put these colored ones in just for looks." He gestured at a sprinkling of antique medicine bottles. "Found most of them colored ones under a wood bridge down toward the lake."

"Have you lived here long?" Kareth asked.

"Not too long. My missus, she got fed up with me and left about a year ago. That was fine with me, but while I was gone one day she had a feller haul off our mobile home. I was real peeved for a while. Then I got to thinking about these bottles. First I built this big room, then the bathroom there. Course, I used all amber glass in there. Privacy, you know."

Kareth nodded, her eyes lit with amusement at this unusual man.

"I set two doors in the wall, one in the front, and one back there. I used those pre-hung ones and just cemented them in the bottles. Now I'm building me a bedroom."

He crossed over to the back door and opened it to

show a waist-high wall of bottles. A red chicken clucked lazily by the gaping doorway.

"I ought to be done with it come winter. As you can see, I made another door. Maybe I'll add me a den back there."

"That's very interesting," Kareth said encouragingly.

"I don't know why more people don't do this," Mr. Cheevey said, puzzled. "It's light when the sun shines and sure won't ever burn down. Mainly, it's free. Gathering bottles by the road does everybody a service."

"I guess nobody ever thought of it before," Kareth suggested tactfully.

"Course, bottles has got hard to find here lately." The man shook his head disparagingly. "Nowadays they use cans." He pointed up. "I flattened a whole drove of them and used them to roof the place. Just nailed them to a wood scaffolding and overlapped them. Worked right good. When I spring a leak I have green beans or carrots for supper and go up there and nail the can over the leak. Course, you want to take off the label first."

"Yes, I imagine that's true."

"Even at that I had a bunch of cans left over." Mr. Cheevey nodded toward a flower arrangement on the small breakfast table. "I used a few on that."

"What?" All she saw were flowers and the table.

"Them flowers there in front of you. I flatten out

them cans and cut out circles of different sizes and spray paint them. Make all kinds of flowers. I got a storage shed nearly full.''

Kareth touched the petals of the flowers she had thought were real zinnias. They were indeed metal. "Why, these are beautiful! Do you sell them?"

Mr. Cheevey scratched his head. "I never thought of that. You reckon anybody would want to buy them?"

"I'm sure they would." Kareth remembered Charley and his camera and tried to take on a more businesslike tone. "Perhaps you could place them on consignment in a store in town."

"Maybe so," he said thoughtfully. "I'll put some thought to that."

After the interview was over, and Charley had packed away the video cam, Mr. Cheevey pointed to the back wall. "I didn't want the young feller taking this down, but what do you think that is you're looking at?" He grinned as if he knew he had her on this one.

Kareth studied the wall. Unlike the other three, all the bottles here were the deep opaque blue of a common medicine bottle, and unlike the other walls, the ends were covered by screw-on lids. "I have no idea," she finally admitted.

Mr. Cheevey chuckled with delight and leaned near so Charley couldn't overhear as he put away the lighting equipment. "That there's my safe."

"What?"

"I ain't got many valuables, just a few family souvenirs and loose change, but I keep it all there in one of those bottles. Course, I sleep right there." He pointed at the single bed. "If a burglar gets in here, I'll hear him before he gets the lids loose and finds the right bottle. Besides, those lids are on real tight. Course, I know how to find the right one. I could go right over there and put my hand on it."

"That's truly incredible," Kareth said with a smile. "Do you worry about burglars out here in the country?"

"No, who would break into a house made out of bottles when there's all those rich houses to rob? No, I'm as safe here as any place in the world."

Kareth told him good-bye and went to her car. Thoughtfully she looked at the small, multicolored house. In his way Mr. Cheevey shared Lake's opinion about theft. Both had locks on the doors and used them, but neither really worried about someone stealing from them. In Los Angeles she had lived in an apartment with three locks on the door and she had been robbed twice. She slowly shook her head. None of it made sense to her.

As she drove back to Livingston she angled out of her way to go to the park that had just been opened. She had not yet had a chance to see how the Merlin looked in its new setting.

She parked in the paved parking area and strolled

beneath the pines and sweet gums. A babble of shrill voices came from the swing area and two older boys raced past her in a game of tag. In passing she spun the child-powered go-round and wished she were still a girl so she could climb up the rope lattice to a tree house. She had always been a bit of a tomboy as a child and that part of her hadn't quite grown up.

Beneath the shade of the trees were concrete picnic tables, most of which were vacant, since it was midafternoon. But on one a squirrel sat eating an orange peel. Kareth stopped to watch for a moment as the squirrel's tiny front feet twirled the peel so its sharp teeth could devour the morsel. As she looked back up she noticed that all the litter cans were full, and already the grounds were strewn here and there with paper plates and soft drink cans. Kareth began to remember why she usually avoided parks.

Ahead she saw the grove of pin oak trees where Lake's statue should be and she quickened her steps. Two more squirrels scattered at her approach and a disturbed blue jay fussed noisily at her. Kareth looked around but saw no sign of the Merlin. Wondering where it could be, she put her hands on her hips and looked more closely. Merlin was seven feet tall and was hardly the sort of thing she could overlook.

She wandered through the trees and came to a dead stop. The center of the grove had been cut and cleared away to form a concrete pavilion that was adjoined by a basketball court. In the middle of the yards of concrete and staring over at the basketball goal was the Merlin.

Slowly Kareth made her feet move forward. This was the Merlin she had seen in the woods beyond Lake's barn and yet it wasn't. Someone had sprayed pale blue paint over the noble features and gesturing hands. The flowing robe no longer seemed to unfurl lightning. It had been hacked and whittled with initials and slogans of dubious merit. Several pigeons perched on Merlin's head, shoulders, and upraised arms. As they flew away Kareth saw they had already done their part in defacing the statue.

Kareth lowered herself in shock to a nearby park bench. The Merlin had been here less than two weeks and already it was ruined. Even the grove of pin oak trees had suffered.

Kareth had suggested this location because of its untouched beauty and now it was destroyed. Tears stung her eyes and she felt as if she were crying for a lost friend.

After a while she could bear it no longer and she left. Perhaps Lake could sand away the blue paint and smooth out the initials, but Merlin would always seem defiled. Bitterly she slammed her car door and wondered whom she should sue in Lake's behalf. The mayor hadn't carved the initials, nor had the park supervisor used the spray paint. The real vandals were long gone and melted into unidentifiable humanity.

Kareth struck the steering wheel with the heel of her hand and muttered an oath at those with such low mentality that they could deface a work of art. That made her feel better, so she did it again, banging unmercifully on the steering wheel.

Rubbing her sore hand, Kareth had to face the obvious. Lake would have to be told. She couldn't let him wander upon his Merlin as she had, or, worse, have it returned to him in that condition without his first being prepared.

Glancing at her watch, Kareth started the car. He was coming to her place tonight and would be there within the hour. With a final glance at the park Kareth drove away.

All the way home she wondered how she would tell him. She couldn't just blurt it out, yet if she prolonged telling him, it might be even worse. What had happened was her fault, even though indirectly, and she felt terrible about it. She parked and walked briskly to her apartment, fit the key into the lock, and went in. She wished she had time to shower. She felt soiled after going to the park, but the clock on her wall reminded her Lake would be there soon.

She stripped off her clothes and tossed them into the hamper, freshened her makeup, and put on a crisp linen blouse in a pale mint color and a skirt of dark green and blue plaid. Tying a sash belt in a double knot around her waist, she stepped into her thin-strapped sandals. She brushed her hair and caught it back with a tortoiseshell clip. Inside she still felt gray and dingy but outside she looked crisp and fresh. She decided that was the best she could hope for.

Going back to the living room, she flopped down on the apricot couch and picked up a novel. The writer was one of her favorites and the story was intriguing, but her mind kept going to the Merlin. She fervently hoped that whoever S.K. and D.A. were, they would be miserable together, along with all the rest of the initial-carvers.

The doorbell rang and she jumped. The book slid out of her hands and she grabbed at it to keep from losing her place. Opening the door, she managed to smile at Lake. "You're late."

"Am I? Sorry about that." He kissed her lightly. "You look terrific. Most people can't wear green."

"Thank you. It's my favorite color. You look nice too," she said inanely. He wore a collared knit pullover in gray and tan and his slacks were charcoal.

"Is something wrong?"

"Why?"

"You usually grab me at the door and kiss me until I can't think straight but tonight you're standing there like a total stranger."

"No. There's nothing wrong. I was just reading and I was surprised when you rang the bell." Lake was so unerringly perceptive. He already knew something was bothering her. It was as if he were reading her mind. She might as well go ahead and tell him. She could just state the facts and have it finished. "Where do you want to eat?" she asked instead.

"How about that barbecue place that just opened on the highway?"

"Cotton-eyed Joe's? That's fine." She paused. This was the time. "I hear the music is good if you like country-western, and I do."

"Me too."

She took her purse from the chair and slipped the shoulder strap in place. At this rate she never would get the words out. Filled with self-loathing, she walked with Lake to his car.

All the way through her meal Kareth tried to find an easy way to tell Lake that his lovely statue was ruined. But he looked at her so lovingly and spoke to her in a way that made every nerve and fiber tingle in her body, and somehow she just couldn't tell him.

"Do you want to dance?" he asked when the waiter had taken away the dishes.

"No, thanks. I'm not up to the schottische tonight," she said. "Do you mind?"

"No." He rested his forearm on the table and regarded her thoughtfully. "Do you want to talk about it?"

"Talk about what?" she demanded, overreacting to the question.

"About whatever it is that's bothering you."

"No, actually I don't. At least not here." If he became as upset as he had every right to be, she didn't want a crowd around for the eruption. People who always seemed to maintain their composure usually came apart at the seams when sufficiently provoked and this would certainly qualify as provoking.

"My place or yours?"

"Mine." She wanted to be on her own turf for this.

They skirted the big dance floor where couples were skipping and kicking to the strains of "Cotton-eyed Joe." Lake paid the cashier and they went out into the cool night.

Kareth inhaled deeply, as if this might be one of her last breaths, and said, "I can still smell the wisterias."

"Soon they'll be finished blooming."

"I guess we'll have a hot summer again this year."

"Of course. All Texas summers are hot. Did you want to give me a weather forecast or is there something else?" He put his arm around her and tried to coax a smile to her lips.

"Let's not talk here."

Lake frowned and opened the car door for her. She was acting pretty strange. When he slid behind the wheel he said, "That man you knew in California hasn't called you, has he?"

"Who?" she asked blankly. Then, "No, no. Nothing like that."

Lake backed the car out and headed toward town. At least no one from her past was bothering her. That left only Chris Merriman and his pending departure. Lake thought of the coming trip. In some ways he was almost looking forward to it. He hadn't traveled in a couple of years and at one time he had enjoyed seeing different parts of the country. Then he had traveled because of his work. But, he reminded himself, this would be work, too. Only now the work had changed to something more enjoyable. Or would it be enjoyable if Kareth weren't there? He kept picturing her beside him in Colorado Springs with its distant wall of mountains or Virginia with the softer, more friendly Blue Ridge or New Mexico with its pastel mesas and flats. Kareth had once said she liked to travel. She was so much a part of his life that he had forgotten again that she wouldn't be accompanying him.

He frowned. Without Kareth he wouldn't want to create and he wouldn't feel free enough to bring unicorns to life from tree stumps. True, he had carved them before he met her, but now that he loved Kareth, she was his inspiration.

"Have you ever considered quitting your job?" he asked abruptly.

"No," she said in surprise. "Why would I want to quit a wonderful job like mine? I even have my own show."

"I just wondered."

Kareth fell silent and for the first time since she had known Lake there was tension in the quietness. Why had he asked her that? she wondered. She had already told him she wanted to keep working if they married and he had agreed. But due to her reticence when he first asked her to marry him, he might not ask again. And, too, she thought dismally, he might not want marriage now with his new career and Chris Merriman.

Again jealousy jabbed her. Never in her entire life had Kareth experienced this emotion. Just the thought of the auburn-haired beauty made her miserable. With a start she realized she had never loved any man enough to fear losing him. Anxiously she glanced at Lake's handsome profile. Was she going to lose him?

Lake maneuvered the car to a stop in the visitor's parking area of Kareth's apartment. Maybe, he thought as he went around to open her door, he could minimize the travel. He had not yet received the contract, so negotiations were still possible. Many woods were the same throughout the country and a Texas pine wasn't vastly different from a Colorado pine. Lake had always been good at contract negotiations and even looked forward to the involved give and take. He had little doubt that he could make this deal more to his advantage, but he had no intention of telling that to Kareth. She had pushed him into this new career surely knowing that it would take him on the road. She had said she needed time to consider his proposal of marriage. Why did she need time? He felt certain she loved him.

He smiled as he walked beside her along the dimly lighted sidewalk. "You look so serious. Are you sure no long-gone lover has surfaced and is trying to get you back?"

"I'm positive. There was only one and he hasn't contacted me since I moved to Texas." She thought of the marred Merlin and wished her troubles were as simple as a persistent ex-lover. Artists were known for their attachment to their work, and rightly so. Lake might well hit a deep depression as soon as his initial wrath passed and it would be all her fault for urging him to expose the Merlin to the public. Somehow she suppressed her groan.

"I did some sketches today for a family of griffins," he said as he took her key and opened the door. "Come out tomorrow and look at them. I've never carved that figure before."

"All right. I'll drive out after work." She watched him close her door and then said, "How about a glass of wine?" He might need a painkiller for her news.

"I'd rather have coffee if it's not too much trouble."

"No trouble at all if you don't mind instant."

"Great." He watched her and wondered why she was acting so distant. "I guess I'll draw up some Merlins too. What do you think about having one large one in each park?" he called to her in the kitchen.

There was a clatter as if she had dropped a cup. "That's entirely up to you," she finally answered in a tight voice.

Lake frowned as he tried to unravel the workings of her mind. Suddenly it all seemed so obvious. Kareth was upset because he wasn't being more enthusiastic. He was amazed this hadn't occurred to him before. She had handed him a television spot with no effort on his part and it had resulted in what anyone else would consider to be a plum of a contract, yet not once had he acted grateful or even thanked her for it. He mentally chastised himself for being a thickheaded fool.

"I really want you to see these sketches," he said, forcing eagerness into his voice. "I thought some dragon pups would be good too. You know, to scatter around the larger dragon. Can you hear me?"

"Yes," she answered in a strained tone. "Dragon babies would be nice."

"I can't thank you enough for giving me this opportunity," he made himself say. "I haven't told you how pleased I am."

He heard the ding of her microwave and soon she reappeared, carrying two cups. "Maybe I'll do more Merlins and sell them to parks all over the country. A Merlin will fit almost any tree trunk, using the lower limbs for arms, so they will be easy to carve. Maybe that could be sort of a trademark of my work. What do you think?"

Kareth made a small noise but smiled shakily.

"How nice." All of a sudden he seemed to want the contract. This was quite an about-face from the attitude he had held earlier and she wondered why he had changed his mind. Still, who wouldn't be flexible when offered money such as he had been promised and Chris Merriman in the bargain. Kareth felt slightly sick. "There's no need to thank me, Lake. Really there isn't."

"But if it weren't for your insistence, none of it would have happened." He sipped his coffee and looked at her. "Is your coffee warm?"

Kareth tasted it. "I must not have left it in the microwave long enough. I'll heat it up." Her mind darted off on tangents. She had been so sure that discovering Lake would be a good move. Now she didn't think so at all. She couldn't recall ever having made a worse mistake.

"This is going to be just great," Lake was saying as she returned the coffee to the microwave. "You never said how you like the idea of me using Merlin as my logo."

"I think that's fine," she said. "Just fine." Going to the door leading from the kitchen to the living room, she said, "Lake, I'm so tired. Would you mind if we say good night?"

"Now? Are you feeling all right?"

"I'm just tired. You wouldn't believe the day I've had today." She found she couldn't tell him about the Merlin after all. Not tonight when he was so filled with enthusiasm for the project.

"Are you sure you're all right?"

"Yes, I just need to be alone. Do you mind?" She didn't need too much perception to figure out that Chris Merriman must have a great deal to do with his burst of excitement over something he had resisted before he met her. "I'm not fit company tonight," she said as she slipped into his arms.

"Everybody needs solitude at times." He hugged her lovingly. "Sometimes I forget that you see people all day and may want to just be alone at night. I understand, honey."

She smiled wanly up at him. "You're a good man, Lake. I guess that's one reason I love you so much."

"I love you too. Get some rest and I'll call you tomorrow."

She nodded and used all her strength not to hurl herself sobbing against his chest. "Is it all right if I drive out after work tomorrow? I'll stop by and pick up hamburgers or something for us to eat."

"That's great. I'll see you tomorrow."

Kareth tilted her head to receive his kiss. "Good night, Lake."

"Good night."

She closed the door after him and leaned her head against the cool wood. With all her heart she longed for him to come back and hold her, but she couldn't ask that without telling him why.

Tomorrow. Then she would find some way to break the news about Merlin. Perhaps it wasn't as bad as she had first thought. She decided to drive back by the park and look at it again.

In the kitchen the microwave beeped and she mechanically went to get out the coffee. Even the handles were hot and bubbles boiled in the steaming liquid. Fatalistically, Kareth closed the door and left the cups where they were. Tomorrow she could pour it out.

She wandered down the short hall to her bedroom and hoped that she would somehow manage to sleep through all of the next day. Then she realized that was highly unlikely.

9

Kareth sat back in her swivel chair and once again read the notes for her next interview. She had read them four times already and didn't know a single word on the page. With an exasperated grimace she tossed the stapled pages onto her cluttered desk. Slouching lower in her chair, she pushed up the mustard-colored sleeve of her loose blouse and rested her chin on her palm.

Without seeing the familiar surroundings, she stared at the wall. Various notes and layouts vied for space with autographed photos of persons she had met or interviewed. In spots the bare cork wall showed through. She had once laughingly referred to her tiny office as a three-dimensional bulletin board.

Her thoughts at the moment were as cluttered and as disorganized as her walls. All too soon Lake would leave for his extended trip to view the park sites. As soon as he returned she assumed he would make more sketches and do whatever it was that he did to prepare to create a sculpture. Then he would fly out again for goodness knows how long to do the actual carving on site.

Kareth took a pencil and multiplied the six sculptures for each park times the six proposed sites. Assuming he flew out only once per carving, he would be gone thirty-six times. And if he did more than one carving at a time, he would be away for months on end.

With a deeper frown she slapped the pencil down onto her desk and bit at the cuticle on her thumb. That was certainly a lot of travel! Realizing what she was doing to her hand, she withdrew it from her mouth.

Over the past weeks she had seen Lake almost every day. If he didn't come to town, she drove out to his place. Now she had to face the prospect of not seeing him for days, weeks, and months at a stretch. Kareth felt a childish rebellion surge within her. She had become spoiled and she wanted the status quo to continue.

Then she recalled Chris Merriman, with her salon-perfect hair, her chic clothes, and her lovely face. Kareth grimaced and again worried her cuticles. The woman was a walking fashion plate! Nobody really looked that good! Nobody except Chris Merriman, and she was to be Lake's companion on all of those trips. Kareth groaned aloud and wished she dared throw something against the wall and indulge herself in a tantrum. All her polished self-control seemed to be melting away.

There was a perfunctory knock and the door opened to admit a short brunette with an abundance of curves. Kareth was already glaring at the door, and the woman paused in mid-stride. "Did I get you at a bad time? Sorry." She started to retreat.

"No, Peg. You didn't disturb me." Kareth softened her glare to a frown. "Do you ever have days when nothing is right and you know it's going to get a lot worse before it improves at all? Well, I've had several of them in a row. You might say I'm really on a roll."

"Sounds bad. Want to talk about it?" Peg came in and closed the door.

Kareth took the papers Peg had brought her and added them to the others on her desk. "Talking won't help. Nothing will. It's hopeless."

"Sounds intriguing. Let's see, you have just heard Halley's comet has changed its course and is heading for Earth? No. The Russians have planted bombs in every building over two stories high all over the country? No. The price is going up again on eggs?"

"No," Kareth said with a slight smile. "It's even worse than higher egg prices, if you can imagine such a thing. I managed to have a friend of mine discovered—he's a sculptor—and he's landed a con-tract that will bring him national recognition."

"Wow! That *is* terrible! Who is this poor guy?" Peg laughed.

"Remember the wood-carver show we did a couple of weeks ago?"

"The hunk that had every woman in the studio drooling?"

"That's the one."

"You're dating him?" Peg exclaimed. "Really?"

"You don't have to sound quite that amazed," Kareth said with a smile. "Actually, we aren't just dating. We love each other."

"So far I don't quite grasp the catastrophe."

"This contract will take him all over the United States. *Thirty-six* trips. I'll scarcely see him!"

"My Jeff travels and I've survived. He's on the road nine months out of the year. You learn to get used to it and after a while it's not bad at all."

"Is that the way you wish it were? I don't want to merely 'get used to it' or to 'survive'! I want to see Lake."

"Yeah," Peg admitted, "I never really got used to it either. I hear wives say they can hardly wait for their husbands to get back on the road and out of their way and I can't help but wonder why they stay married if they really feel that way. Jeff tells me he has to travel until he has enough seniority to get a desk job, but I think he enjoys it. Shoot, even when he's in town he's off fishing or hunting. It's something wives have to put up with."

"Why?" Kareth demanded.

"I don't know why. I guess because we always have."

"Not me," Kareth said stubbornly. "I want a man who will give our relationship priority over his job."

"Lots of luck," Peg scoffed. "I'm not sure that man has been born yet."

Kareth riffled disconsolately through some papers. "What really gets me is that I almost forced him into this. No, I *did* push him to accept the contract."

"Now I'm beginning to see. Not only is he going to travel, it's your fault. Heavy."

"What am I going to do? I love him and I want to marry him, but I'm too selfish to want him to pursue his career. I'm a terrible person!" Suddenly Kareth realized what she had said. She *did* want to marry him and she wasn't sure when she had stopped fighting the idea.

"No, you're just in love. Everybody goes a little wacky at that time."

"I think I'm more than wacky. I may be certifiably insane." Kareth rechecked her inner feelings for the panic which usually came to the fore at just the thought of marriage, and found only a calm, reassuring sense of peace.

Peg just smiled back at her. "It's almost quitting time. Why don't you leave early? Mr. Alred has gone for the day."

"I don't know," Kareth said in a bewildered tone. "I have all this work that I still haven't finished."

"It'll still be here tomorrow." Peg smiled and motioned toward the door. "You aren't going to get anything done at the rate you're going."

"I think you're right." Kareth stood up and slipped on her white blazer and smoothed her tan and chocolate striped skirt. "I'll try to come in early tomorrow." As she passed Peg she said, "Thanks for letting me talk. It did help after all."

Peg grinned. "It always does. And Kareth, good luck on your new way of marriage. Maybe if anyone achieves it, word will get around to less enlightened men."

Kareth made a thumbs-up sign and grabbed her purse. "See you tomorrow."

She walked down the narrow hall and out the exit to the parking lot. While she felt better for having told someone of her quandary, she was despondent over Peg's fatalism—especially since she knew Peg was right about the way most marriages went. The best jobs usually involved some, or even a lot, of travel. Wives were universally expected to smile and accept it and to keep a light in the window and food on the stove in preparation for the husband's return, even if the wives also worked and had the added responsibility of children to raise. This double standard was another of the reasons Kareth had never married.

She drove out to the park and left her car by the basketball court. All day she had tried to block out images of the ravaged Merlin. Before she went to Lake's house she had to see if it was as bad as she had first thought.

As she approached the large carving she saw it wasn't quite as she had recalled. Since the previous day "Vickie loves Tommy" had been added to Merlin's flowing sleeve, along with a heart proclaiming Tommy's undying devotion to Dee Dee.

Kareth stood in front of Merlin and gazed miserably at the pigeons that eyed her warily from the poised hands. The longer Merlin stood here, the worse the damage would be.

Resolutely she went to the pay phone by the rest rooms and called the mayor's office. When the nasal-toned secretary informed her the mayor had left for the day, Kareth left a terse message that would most likely be heavily edited before it reached the mayor.

Shouldering her bag, Kareth stalked back to her car and screeched out of the parking place. She drove automatically, her thoughts not on the road but on her predicament. Why, she demanded of herself, hadn't she left well enough alone? Why had she barged in and disrupted Lake's peaceful life? With new insight she saw that Lake was like the Merlin. In his element he was at ease, in command, even godlike, but set in the wrong surroundings Lake might be just as vulnerable as his creation.

With a groan Kareth pressed the accelerator down and left Livingston in her rearview mirror. She had always had a knack for complicating her life, but this time she had botched up someone else's as well.

She reached the log house and parked beneath the sprawling oak tree. Lake sat sketching on the porch and he waved as she got out of the car.

"Come look at this," he called as he worked. "I may do some winged cats."

Kareth slowly crossed the grass and mounted the steps. Looking over his shoulder, she saw a puma he had drawn. It had a wiry grace and angellike wings, and a snarl that revealed long, curving fangs.

"I don't see any reason to stick with the animals I've already carved," Lake said as he finished shading a sinewy shoulder. "What do you think?"

"I like it."

Lake lifted his head and regarded her thoughtfully. "Are you still in that down mood? What's going on?"

"Your Merlin is ruined," she blurted out.

"My what?" He sat perfectly still, his charcoal pencil held at a slant in his fingers.

"The Merlin you loaned the park. The mayor promised it would be protected but it wasn't." Her voice broke and she looked away. "Oh, Lake, I feel so terrible about this!"

"Honey, don't cry. Come sit on the swing." He led her over and sat down beside her. After a bit he said, "Is it really bad?"

She nodded tearfully. "It really is. There's spray paint and initials and the pigeons have—"

"Spare me the rest." A small muscle knotted in his jaw. "I was afraid this would happen."

"And now you're going to do others to go in all those amusement parks! I hadn't thought of that!"

"They will be under a strict security guard," he said absently. "Besides, for the price Chris is paying, I could hardly complain if they are burned to the ground. The Merlin, though, that's a real blow. It's funny," he said without looking at her. "I knew I shouldn't have put it on loan and I did it anyway. I wonder if I'll ever learn to listen to my hunches."

"I'm so sorry," Kareth said, laying her hand on his arm. "If I had had any idea this would happen, I would never have suggested it. Can you put it back the way it was?"

"Not if it's as bad as you say. I can sand it but it won't be the same."

"I'm so sorry," she repeated again.

"Well," he said in an effort to salvage the evening, "I received the contract today and have started negotiations."

"Have you?" Kareth said, her face threatening to crumble.

"There are a few things I don't agree with, but in general it's pretty straightforward."

"I added it up today and I figure you will be gone thirty-six times."

"No, not nearly that many."

"No?"

"According to the contract, when Chris said she

wanted native woods, she really meant it. I'm to go and live on site."

"Live there!" Kareth gasped.

"She's arranging for me to have an apartment in Colorado Springs. That will be the first location to open."

"Apartment! Colorado Springs!"

"There's a terrible echo on this porch," Lake commented dryly.

"You want to move away?" Kareth demanded. The idea of his traveling so much had been bad enough, but this toppled her self-pity over into anger. "I thought when she said lodging she meant you would stay in a motel! You want to move to Colorado Springs? With Chris?" Jealousy sparked her anger past reasonableness.

"What do you mean with Chris? No, I don't want to leave here and move anywhere! It's just that shipping entire trees from Colorado to Texas seems out of the question! What are you getting so mad about? I thought this was what you wanted."

"Oh, sure you did!" Kareth snapped as she stood up, the swing jouncing behind her.

"Well, it was all your idea!" Lake leaped to his feet, sending the swing wagging crazily. "You're the one who wheedled me into being on your show and then insisted I take this contract!"

"I never wheedled! I've never done such a thing in my life. How dare you say I wheedled!"

"Then when I agreed to talk to Chris, you acted as

my business manager. You even talked her into paying twice her original offer!" He glared at her as if this were somehow a fault.

"Chris, Chris, Chris! That's all I've heard since I got here. I'm beginning to wonder if the contract is nearly as interesting to you as the woman who sent it!"

"That is absolutely ridiculous!"

"Is it? Then call it all off!"

"I will not! She came all the way out here and she likes my work. You said yourself that this is the chance of a lifetime. What about my 'debt to art'? Have you forgotten about that?"

"Don't throw my words back at me! I know what I said and what I meant when I said them. I did *not* say you should follow that . . . that mannequin to Colorado in order to fulfill your art!"

"You sound like a damn museum guide. 'Fulfill my art!' Hell, all I wanted to do was carve trees in my own yard. *You're* the one who insisted I become a national figure."

"And now I've changed my mind!"

"It's too late. I've agreed to do the work."

Kareth battled hard to control her fury and her tongue. Both, however, were out of control. "You mean you've agreed to compromise yourself for Chris Merriman!"

Dead silence reigned on the porch. At last Lake spoke in a deathly calm voice, "Why do I get the feeling you had a word in mind other than *compromise?*"

Kareth's chin jerked up angrily. "You tell me, Lake. Is that what's happening?"

Rage warred within him and flashed in the jade depths of his eyes. "I've given you no reason to be jealous," he finally ground out. "Chris means no more to me than any other business contact."

"Will you be seeing her?"

"Since she has hired me to carve on site, I assume I will see her daily."

"I see." Kareth's voice was frigid. "And how long will it take before this . . . project . . . is finished?"

He glared at her before he said, "The dragon by the bridge took three months, the unicorn over two months. At six carvings for each park, I will work about a year and a half on each location."

Kareth gasped. "Years! I thought you said you work fast!"

"That *is* fast! I've had friends say that dragon would have taken them a year!"

"For one sculpture!"

"Where did you get the idea I could just whip out these carvings in the bat of an eye? I'm working with hard wood, not soap bars!"

Kareth stared at him in anguish. "How long," she croaked. "How long before you're finished?"

"Nine years total time for all six parks as near as I can tell, but—"

"Nine years! Call it off!" Kareth interrupted.

"I can't do that! I gave my word!"

"Lake, you'll be gone *nine years!*"

"With Chris," he goaded. "Don't forget her." Like most people who are slow to anger, once aroused Lake fought with every weapon at hand. Even those that also wounded the user.

Kareth's eyes grew large and pain flashed in them. "No," she was able to say. "I can't forget Chris."

Turning abruptly, she hurried off the porch and across the yard. Lake called after her, but she ignored him. Tears were streaming down her face and she fled before he could hurt her any more than he had, if that were even possible. A clammy fist seemed to be clenched around her heart and she had to struggle to breathe.

Her car spun out of the yard, leaving handfuls of bluebonnets in clumps in her trail. It fishtailed on the dirt drive as she struggled to regain control before she shot out onto the black-topped farm road. Glancing at the house, she saw Lake in the yard, where she had been parked. Even his stance proclaimed his anger. Kareth pressed the accelerator and sped down the road.

Rather than going home she drove to the lake. She had found this place during an afternoon's idleness and she had never seen another person there. She crossed two cattle guards and rolled to a stop by the blue-green water. Across the water she could see a marina and the peaked roof of a restaurant. Here there were only willows, grass, and a few white-faced cows to share her solitude.

She got out of the car and wandered down to the water. A cloud of gnats hovered over the clear surface, and minnows swam beneath, waiting for a chance to gulp down a gnat. Kareth sat on an uprooted willow and stared sightlessly at the water.

How could Lake have said those things to her? How could she have said them to him? Love meant not hurting the one you adored, or at least she had always thought so. Did it also mean seeing the dark side of love at times? If she could hurt in direct proportion to the amount she could love, then this was an awesome fact indeed.

She dangled a twig in the water and a series of concentric circles spread. Minnows gathered around the submerged tip in hopes it might be food, then flicked away.

Although her chest still ached and her throat was tight from unshed tears, Kareth didn't love Lake any less. She wished she did because she doubted he ever wanted to see her again, but she still loved him as much as ever. Maybe, she thought, this had happened at the best time. The love between them blazed so bright and with such a white heat that perhaps it was fated to burn itself out. At least, she tried to philosophize, they hadn't gotten married and then had the burnout.

The only trouble was that she didn't feel any less love for him than she ever had. New tears rose and overflowed down her cheeks. Kareth sat by the lake and cried until sunset bruised the sky.

Exhausted from her torment, she went home. With trepidation she groped about in the darkness of her living room until she found the lamp. She switched it on and closed the front door. As she locked the dead bolt she wished she could lock away her thoughts and emotions as easily.

As tiny as her apartment was, it seemed to be cavernous in her state of loneliness. Kareth went to the kitchen and poured herself a glass of milk in lieu of dinner. Sipping it slowly and telling herself she liked milk, though she never had, Kareth turned on the hall light and went to her bedroom.

She sat on her bed and looked around at the room. The same rose-hued curtains, the familiar rose and scarlet bedspread, the usual four walls and furniture. Had it always been so small, so empty? Kareth drained her glass and wrinkled her nose at the opaque residue of the milk.

"I hate milk," she confirmed solemnly.

Her voice sounded loud in the silent apartment and that made her more lonely for Lake. She mentally ran through their argument and tried to find some way she could have averted it or ended it with her in his arms. At once she saw a dozen ways she could have done either and this made her even more miserable.

She went back to the kitchen and washed the

glass. Then she turned out the lights and went back to the bedroom. Although her watch said it was only nine o'clock, Kareth undressed and put on her favorite nightgown, an old cotton one that had seen her through many personal traumas. She picked up a book, then tossed it back onto the dresser. This was no time to lose herself in fiction; her own life was beginning to sound like a bad melodrama.

Turning back the covers, she lay down and switched off the lamp. The room was plunged into darkness and she remembered another time when the room had been even blacker, with an electrical storm raging overhead. She looked at the drawn curtains, where the outside security light made a dappled silver pattern and softened the darkness. That night Lake had lit candles and had loved her until she would never be quite the same person again.

The pain of losing him ripped at her and she shut her eyes tight. She would stop torturing herself! She would!

Although she didn't feel like watching television, she turned on the set and propped herself up on both pillows. Her thoughts still skittered through her head, but she forced herself to watch the bright pictures on the screen. Shadows flickered around the dark room and the show's audio was only a meaningless jumble of sound to her.

Once she thought she heard someone at her door

and she sat bolt upright expectantly, but she realized it must have been the television.

After lying back down she rolled her head to look at the silent phone. All she had to do was dial Lake's number. Then he could twist another knife into her heart and she would be worse off than she was.

Kareth reached over and unplugged the phone as a gesture of defiance. She wasn't going to call him! She was no glutton for punishment.

She resolutely glued her eyes to the small screen and tried to lose herself in a commercial for Chow Chows, the banquet dinner for dogs. She was expecting the night to be tediously long.

As she had expected, it was hours before she fell asleep, and even then she only dozed fitfully.

The next morning she decided to swallow her pride. But when she tried to call Lake, there was no answer. Nor was there all that day or the next. She eventually had to accept the fact that he was gone. And he had not said good-bye.

10

Lake nodded in absentminded agreement as Chris showed him the placement of the runaway sleigh ride. At the moment there was only a tangle of poplar and brush. She was explaining that the poplars could be cut for the wood he needed, as well as a large pine.

He nodded and put his hand on the rough bark. "I can get a Merlin out of this pine and maybe a fairy. Before it's cut I want to mark it so it's not sawn in the wrong place. The same goes for the poplars."

"What do you think about the park so far?" Chris asked.

"I like it. You've put a lot of planning into it. It's close to both Denver and Colorado Springs, but is off the main road. That will cut down on impulse visitors, but driving into the countryside will lend the park more atmosphere."

"That's exactly what I thought." Chris shaded her pale green eyes and gazed at the distant mountains. Her auburn hair was caught back with barrettes and she wore tan slacks and a camel-and-rust-striped blouse. A tan sweater was knotted loosely around her shoulders. As usual she looked as if she had just stepped off a magazine cover. "I plan to put the merry-go-round over there by the stream."

"Maybe instead of the usual horses, you should get unicorns and griffins," Lake suggested, trying to get into the spirit of things. He was finding it very difficult to keep his mind on work. He only wanted to try once more to call Kareth as he had at every opportunity for the past two days. Every time he tried she wasn't at the station or no one answered her home phone.

"Unicorns and griffins! What a lovely idea," Chris said enthusiastically. "You're right. The theme should be used throughout. Would you consider carving them? I doubt they would be available anywhere else."

"Maybe." He wished he hadn't mentioned that. Now he would have even more work to do.

"I'll increase your commission accordingly. I'd like figures for all six merry-go-rounds."

"I can do it, but not in time for the opening. Carving that many figures will take over a year, maybe two, for each park."

"So long?"

"I suggest you start off with a conventional merry-go-round and add the fantasy figures when they're finished."

"A good idea. The tunnel of love should also carry out the theme. Maybe boats with swans heads and wings."

Lake scarcely listened. Under the guise of paying attention he studied Chris. She was attractive, but he thought Kareth was much more so. Kareth's beauty seemed to come to her very naturally, while he suspected Chris relied on her makeup brush for her good looks. Lake had never really objected to women who used obvious makeup techniques, especially if it was done artfully, but it wasn't the look he preferred. He enjoyed Chris's company and he found her receptive to his ideas, but all his dealings with her were entirely businesslike. Not once had there been even the slightest suggestion of a sexual current between them. He couldn't for the life of him see why Kareth had been so jealous.

Lake gazed around at the wooded acres and imagined how it would look with shady paths, various rides, and his statues. He was pleased with the project. "I like your idea," he said approvingly.

"For the swan boats?"

"All of it. The more I hear about it, the better it sounds."

Chris beamed with pleasure. "I'm glad to hear you say that. I value your opinion. I can hardly believe my luck in finding a sculptor of your merit to do the carvings.''

Thoughtfully Lake walked by her to inspect the stream. He had to admit that he had enjoyed the ego boost of being "discovered," but now that the first blush was over, he was beginning to realize the amount of work he was facing.

Also there was the obvious drawback of having to live on site. He liked Colorado, and always had, but his home was in Texas. With Kareth.

He wondered what she was doing. When she hadn't answered her phone after their argument, he had driven to town only to find her apartment dark. He had knocked but when she didn't come to the door he had assumed she had gone to a friend's house. Since he knew Peg's first name only and Kareth had never mentioned another close friend, Lake had had no choice but to go home.

His flight had left at noon from Houston the next day and only the television station receptionist's solemn promise that Kareth had shown up for work saved him from blind panic. Her work kept her out interviewing quite a bit and it was possible that she really wasn't at the station when he called. It was also possible that she had left word at the switchboard that she didn't want to talk to him. He was sure the phone was unplugged in her apartment because he had had the operator check to see if the line was working. No one could be gone so consistently.

This brought the recurrent ache to his heart. He

missed her so very much. Even more than he had thought he could. He had made a few preliminary sketches but the figures seemed stiff and awkward. Without Kareth he couldn't seem to create whimsical animals full of life and grace. She had captured a part of him and held it enthralled. He wondered painfully if she would ever speak to him again. She had been furious when she drove away—and with good reason.

Lake's jaw clenched as he recalled what he had said. A soured marriage had taught him all he needed to know about fighting dirty, but Kareth wouldn't realize that. She might have even believed he meant all those things he had said! He assumed she knew him better than that, but he couldn't find her in order to be sure.

Chris, totally oblivious to the anguish he was feeling, nodded toward a straight stretch of stream. "I'll build a bridge here. One of those curving ones that looks like a rainbow. Maybe there should be three or four scattered up and down the stream. They could be painted in rainbow colors. I have received permission to widen the river beds so that the stream stays in the banks and is more of a small river. I think the park's encompassing fence should be woven of reeds fixed to a firmer support. I dislike seeing boundaries at an amusement park, don't you?"

With a nod Lake walked back with her toward the rental car

"The front gate should be something to bring out the child in everyone." She looked around critically, seeing the place not as it was, but as it would be.

"How about entering through a dragon's mouth?" Lake ventured. "A big one with fangs two feet long? The tongue could be the walkway."

"Perfect! There might even be a way to shoot smoke out through his nostrils!" She glanced at him admiringly. "Your ideas are brilliant. It's easy to see you've always lived an artist's life. The child in you is still alive and well."

Lake laughed. "You might be surprised."

"The only trouble is the expense," Chris said almost to herself. "All this is growing by leaps and bounds. Not that I'll have any trouble in paying you," she reassured him hastily, "but the costs are mounting. I'm afraid I'm a perfectionist and I don't like to settle for less than the best. Now that you've mentioned the dragon-mouth gate, I'll never be happy with a plain ticket booth."

"Would you consider taking a partner?" Lake asked.

"Who would want to come in on my plan at this late date? I've already signed contracts for the first of the parks and I wouldn't welcome an outsider's opinions."

"The partner I was suggesting would be a silent one. He would supplement your finances and in return get a share of the eventual profit. For certain concessions."

"Such as?" Chris demanded suspiciously.

"Let's talk on our way to the airport. Our flight leaves in two hours and we can discuss this on our way to Virginia. I'm pretty sure we can work out something advantageous to us both."

Kareth regarded the woman in the chicken costume and tried to keep her mind on business. "I would like to interview you on my show, Mrs. Nibbets. Your occupation is certainly unusual." She ducked to avoid a cloud of silver balloons.

"Yeah, don't I know it?" The shorter woman let helium screech from the tank into another balloon and the sound seemed to echo in the small warehouse. "And I want to do it. Here. Hold these balloons, will you? As you can see, I'm late for that kid's party. It's like this all the time. I could still use the free advertising though." She peered at Kareth from under the bright orange beak. "It is free, isn't it?"

"Well, yes, but I would like to focus the story on why you chose this line of work rather than the work itself."

"It takes a crazy person to do this. Do you know how hot a chicken suit gets in the summer? It's a wonder real chickens don't baste in their own juices. Hand me that string."

Kareth found a ball of twine and passed it to the woman. "If it's so hot, why are you wearing it now?"

"I have to have help getting into this thing. My

assistant had to leave early—a sick kid at home—and I had to dress before she left. Whew, I'm burning up!'' She fanned her feathers ineffectually. ''My assistant was supposed to blow these balloons up but she didn't. Can't trust her to do anything right.''

Kareth tightened her hold on the helium-filled balloons and juggled her writing pad into position to take notes.

''Hey, don't turn loose those strings! They'll go straight to the ceiling and I'll never get them down.''

The ceiling of the metal warehouse was nearly two stories up. Kareth gripped the strings firmly. ''Why did you decide to open Balloons for All?''

''I needed the money. Got tired of clerking and decided to go into business on my own.''

''I gather you like children?'' Kareth encouraged as she scribbled quickly.

''Not especially. Their parents do, though, and that means loot in my pocket. I do other parties too. I've got some black balloons I deliver to people turning thirty or forty. Office workers usually order them. I throw in a batch of withered flowers and dress up like an old crone. It's a real gas.''

''Sounds delightful,'' Kareth said in an unconvinced tone. She was beginning to have second thoughts about Mrs. Nibbets's suitability for her show. ''Are you native to this area?''

''Naw. That makes me sound like a hybrid tomato or something. My husband moved me to Texas and

I've been trying to get out ever since. Can you help me get these balloons to my van?"

Kareth closed her notebook. Her eyes were decidedly cool now. "Yes, I can do that."

She followed the giant chicken outside to a gray and blue van. The woman unlocked the back door and climbed in. "If I'm going to be on television, I want to mention my prices," she cautioned Kareth. "If I'm doing this appearance for free, I might as well get something out of it. Right?"

"This isn't a commercial spot, Mrs. Nibbets. I want to interview you, not act as free advertising." Kareth's head throbbed dully and she wanted only to leave.

"Yeah, well, I gotta think about it."

"It may be a while before I contact you. As I told you earlier, I'm already lining up shows for next month."

"With any kind of luck I won't be doing this that long. That husband of mine is getting a transfer or else!" She scowled at Kareth from within the feathered suit. "Spending hours with screaming kids isn't my idea of fun."

"I see." Kareth's face felt like cardboard from disguising her emotions.

"Hey, don't crimp the strings like that. Give me the balloons."

Kareth would never know if what happened next was a result of clumsiness or subconscious retaliation, but as Mrs. Nibbets reached for the handful of balloons, they were caught in a sudden gust of air and went sliding between their fingers. Mrs. Nibbets let out a squawk that did credit to her strange garb. Kareth stared in amazement as the dozens of silver balloons wafted up over the metal building and into the sky.

Kareth apologized profusely but beat a hasty retreat to her car. Mrs. Nibbets followed her every step of the way, waving her feathered arms and screeching imprecations.

When she was safely on the road Kareth heaved a sigh of relief. Not everyone she interviewed was right for the show, but this one had been a really bad mistake. She grimaced at the tiny clutch of balloons that were barely visible above her rearview mirror. The most she could hope for from this interview would be that Mrs. Nibbets wouldn't demand that the station pay for her ruined appearance.

Not that Kareth was really surprised at the way her day was shaping up. Since Lake had gone none of her days were all that great. A deep depression nudged her and she tried to overcome it. If she meant no more to him than that, she was well rid of him. She only wished she could believe that.

This was the same highway that intersected the farm-to-market road by Lake's house. As she neared the turnoff she automatically slowed. She shouldn't drive by. That was more the style of a teenager than a mature woman. A quick glance at her watch told her she had time and she turned down the familiar black-topped road.

Her pulse quickened as his house came into sight. His car wasn't visible and the yard was deserted, as she had known it would be. Detesting herself for her weakness, Kareth went up the curving dirt drive and stopped under the oak tree.

The cobalt blush of the bluebonnets was gone now with the passage of time and instead, the yard was lush with greenery. The swing hung empty at one side of the front porch and at the other end she saw the grouping of lawn chairs where she and Lake had often sat and talked. They had had so much to say to each other. She recalled dates during which they had both seemed to talk nonstop. How had it ended so abruptly?

Almost against her will Kareth got out of the car and strolled over the yard, where they had tumbled and loved in happy abandon. She had no business being here and she knew it. Technically she was trespassing and emotionally she was doing much worse. Her steps slowed and she gazed at the house. There was a good chance she would never see it again. Probably Lake would rent it out when he moved to location and then she couldn't come here again and torment herself.

Feeling she deserved a good-bye from the place she had come to love, she wandered toward the path to the bridge. Seeing the carvings one last time wouldn't hurt, she reasoned, and she wasn't due at the station for nearly an hour.

The deep shade closed over her and even though the blossoms on the dogwoods and wisteria had vanished for another year, she was reminded of her first walk through these woods. A feeling of magic seemed inherent in the trees and bushes, making her feel welcome and unafraid. Their timeless calm soothed her and made her want never to leave.

The small bridge lay ahead and she mounted it almost reverently. The troll with its malevolent little smile crouched in the cool shadows by the stream. Rain had swollen the water from its normal trickle to a full course. She put her palms on the cedar railing and looked down at her reflection. A memory rose from childhood of Walt Disney's Snow White, where the prince's reflection appeared beside the girl's. But this was reality and she remained alone.

Looking over at the dragon coiled between the redbud saplings, Kareth wondered if Lake would insure the carvings before he put his house up for rent. Her disaster with the Merlin had shaken what little faith she had in people in general. Knowing Lake, however, she guessed he wouldn't bother. He held stubbornly to the idea of objects being invincible when they were in their proper surroundings. Kareth smiled as she realized she had almost started believing it herself.

Not much farther down the path was the small

clearing where she had first met Lake, where it had all begun. Kareth hesitated for a moment as the memory of that meeting came into sharp focus, then blurred and began to fade. Quickening her step in hopes of recapturing the images, she moved into the clearing. Just as before, the birds sang and leaves shimmered in the breeze, but the principal objects were frozen in a moment of time—the unicorn surprised in drinking, the fairies in their forever game of leapfrog. And Lake, standing beside a new carving of a woman that bore a remarkable resemblance to herself.

Her breath caught in her throat and she stared at him with eyes as startled as a fawn's. He stared back as if he, too, could hardly believe they were together.

Embarrassed at being caught on his land, Kareth turned to run away.

"Don't go!" Lake called out.

She hesitated, then said, "I didn't think you would be here."

"I got home an hour ago. I tried to call you at the station but as usual they said you weren't there. I guess this time you really weren't."

" 'As usual'?"

"I've tried to find you ever since you left me. I was going to wait until it was time for you to leave work today and try to catch you before you left."

"I've been busy lately." She had tried to stay occupied in order to keep him off her mind.

"If I missed you at the station I was going to go to

your apartment and wait on your doorstep until you came home. I've been worried sick over you."

"Lake, why are you here? Why aren't you flying from spot to spot or moving into your new place in Colorado?"

"I've seen the park sites and I have plenty of notes to start on my carvings. Right here. I'm not moving."

"You're not?" She took a hesitant step toward him.

"No, I'm not. I've given it a lot of thought. I tried it your way and I didn't like it. My place is here, not in an apartment somewhere else. I've decided to do it my way and you'll just have to put up with it."

"I will?"

"I'm not going to 'further my career' or 'pay my dues to art' unless that just happens to come about naturally. The rat race isn't for me."

"Then you turned Chris down?"

"No, the wood will be shipped to me here and after the statues are finished I'll ship them back to her."

"But that will be terribly expensive! Did Chris agree to this?"

"She sure did. You're now looking at her business partner. I bought into Merriman Industries."

"Oh, Lake," Kareth protested. "You didn't! Did

she take advantage of you? That must mean you will see no profit at all on your sculpture! Have you signed anything?"

"Slow down," he said, dropping his wood chisel and coming to her. "I keep telling you I don't need the money."

"Everybody needs money!"

"Before you get mad again, listen to me. I already *have* money."

"But—"

"Have you ever heard of Johnston Enterprises?"

"Of course. They own a chain of motels and restaurants. So what?"

"My mother's maiden name was Johnston. I sold the company when I left Houston but I kept the controlling interests. I really *do* have all the money I need. Or that you will need, or a whole houseful of babies."

"You're Johnston Enterprises?"

"That's right. And Merriman Industries as of yesterday."

"Damn you! You're rich! You never told me that!"

"It's not something you tell every stranger you meet. Later I tried to tell you, but you wouldn't listen to me."

"But you signed the contract to do all that work. Why?"

"Because it was obviously very important to you. And after I thought about it some, I guess my ego swelled. I've never had someone compliment me so highly before."

"But you could have tried harder to tell me you had money. If you knew how often I've worried about you—I had you practically starving in a gutter! Now I find out you own the gutter and plan to turn it into a shopping center!"

He shrugged. "I like to live simply. Everything I want is right here. And that's another thing—we're getting married."

"What!"

"I tried asking nicely and you said you loved me but no thanks. I've decided you don't know what you want. Ever since I left I've been in agony from wanting you and wondering if you were all right. Now I find you out here and I can only assume you still feel something for me."

"You have no problem with self-doubt, do you!"

Lake took the last step toward her and gathered her into his embrace. Before she could protest he kissed her, drawing a response from deep within them both.

Kareth didn't remember putting her arms around him, but she held him tightly, as if she would never let him go. Her mouth moved with his and their bodies molded together in a perfect match.

"Marry me," he commanded shakily.

"And have you think you can order me about from now on? Forget it."

Again his lips captured and conquered hers. She felt his tongue exploring her mouth and she met it eagerly with her own. As she did, his hand found her breast and caressed it lovingly. Since that day she had told Peg she wanted to marry Lake, Kareth had been certain of her feelings for him, but if she had had any doubts, the passion he stirred in her would have laid them to rest.

"Marry me," he demanded again. "Say you'll marry me!"

"And interrupt such a convincing argument? No way."

He gazed down at her, not sure if she was teasing or not. Kareth grinned up at him mischievously and pulled his head back down for her kiss.

This time she was the one to say, "Marry me. As soon as possible, before I pull some other stupid stunt and send you off to carve in India or somewhere!"

"I won't go. What we have together is far more important than any career."

She leaned back and looked incredulously at him, then caught him close in an exuberant bear hug. Her miracle had happened! He had put her at the top of his priority list!

"Does that mean you really will marry me?" he asked in confusion. "You still love me even after that fight?"

"I never stopped loving you," she whispered

happily. "I could stop breathing easier than I could quit loving you."

Lake held her close and buried his face in her thick hair. "I love you, Kareth. I always will."

All around them the forest spun its spell of enchantment, and Kareth began to believe in happily ever after.

COMING NEXT MONTH

MAN'S BEST FRIEND
Amanda York

Unshaven, uncombed and definitely untidy, Will O'Keefe had a face even a mother couldn't describe as handsome. But his charm and his appeal were undeniable, and despite her careful plans, Alex knew she had to follow her heart. Every dog has his day, and this was theirs.

ANGEL IN HIS ARMS
Suzanne Carey

Fate led Annie Duprez to Bourbon Street and into the arms of Jake St. Arnold. It was black magic from the first. Yet the past hung over them, an unanswered question with the power to force them apart. Did Annie have the strength to face the truth, even if it meant losing the man she loved?

LOVE LETTERS
Elaine Camp

The publicity for her first book was being handled by her old college buddy Whit Hayes, but Emmy felt differently about Whit now. If only he'd stop deluging her with roses!

COMING NEXT MONTH

RED TAIL
Lindsay McKenna

Flying together gave them an intimacy soon strengthened by their growing need for each other when they were on the ground. Bram's passion unleashed her innermost needs, but Storm knew she was flying blind over dangerous waters.

FOOL'S GOLD
Beverly Bird

Clay didn't trust women without money. Devon knew he wouldn't believe it was his personality, not his bank balance, that drew her. And even if he did, there was another problem to deal with: the fact that she'd run out on him — fast — right after their first magical meeting.

THAT SPECIAL MAGIC
Laurien Blair

She loved health food, exercise, the outdoors. He loved pizza, beer and city living. When the two started fiercely protecting their own lifestyles, their love affair became a test of wills.

All it needed was…that special magic.

OCTOBER TITLES